The Legacy's World

Steampunk OZ: Book 2

by Steve DeWinter

I0625848

Summary

There is no yellow brick road here. No emerald city. No lollipop guild. This is the Australis Penal Colony, a continent sized prison referred to the world over as the Outcast Zone. Built to contain the world's most dangerous criminals, OZ ended up the dumping ground for everything polite society deemed undesirable.

Book 2

Dorothy's sudden, and violent, entry into OZ puts her into a position of power. Power she will need if she hopes to find her father in a place more dangerous than she has ever experienced before.

Ramblin' Prose Publishing
Copyright © 2014 Steve DeWinter
All rights reserved. Used under authorization.
www.stevedw.com

eBook Edition
ISBN-10: 1-61978-034-8
ISBN-13: 978-1-61978-034-7

Paperback Edition
ISBN-10: 1-61978-035-6
ISBN-13: 978-1-61978-035-4

Chapter 1

It was pitch black.

So this is this what death's like, thought Dorothy.

She moved slightly and felt the muscles in her face twitch as she grimaced from the pain.

No, she couldn't be dead. You weren't supposed to feel anything once you were dead.

And right now, every muscle ached.

She could hear faint voices all around her.

"Do you think she will be better than the last Marshal?"

"Anybody would be better than her."

"What about her sister? What do you think she will do when she finds out?"

Dorothy's eyes fluttered open and it was no longer pitch black.

A wrinkled face moved into her field of view.

"She's awake."

More tiny wrinkled faces moved into view all around her.

One of the faces smiled, showing only three teeth in the bottom row and no teeth in the top row. "How are you feeling?"

She tried to speak, but her throat refused to respond and she coughed instead.

Smiley looked over his shoulder. "Bring her some water."

A stubby hand took the back of her head and lifted her up to meet the dented tin cup that appeared before her.

"Drink. It will make you feel better."

Dorothy hadn't realized how thirsty she was as she gulped at the rusty tasting water. Her throat soothed, she could finally sit up and look around her.

She was sitting in a tiny bed, her legs dropping over the bottom edge with plenty of room for her feet to touch the floor.

The men gathered around her were no more than three or four feet tall. Their dingy clothing all the same color of gray. They all smiled at her.

"Where am I?"

Smiley stepped forward and bowed. "You are a most honored guest in my home. My name is

Munch." He opened his arms wide, indicating all the other short men around him. "And these are my brothers."

"How did I get here?"

"Your ship crashed into the center of town. We brought you here and tended to your injuries."

She looked down at the bandage around her arm. "How long…"

Munch smiled again, the lack of teeth even more evident. "You are welcome to stay as long as you like."

"Oh, hell no!" Dorothy swung her feet over to the side and grimaced with the pain. "I am not your Snow White."

Munch frowned. "Who?"

She shook her head. "Never mind. I meant, how long have I been asleep?"

"All of yesterday, most of the night and half of the morning."

"I have to go."

"Of course, you must begin your duties as Marshal."

"My what?"

"Your Marshal duties."

"My Marshal duties? Where am I?"

"You are home."

Dorothy looked around her. "I'm back in New Kansas?"

"No, you are in OZ."

Dorothy cleared the cobwebs from her brain with a shake of her head.

"That's right. I crashed in the Outcast Zone?"

Munch grimaced. "We like to call it OZ. Sounds less depressing."

She pulled back the covers and stood up. The room tilted wildly and she sat back down hard on the bed.

"Don't try to get up Marshal. You are still weak from your arrival."

She held her head until the room slowed down enough for her to focus on the one called Munch. At least she thought that one was Munch. Every one of these little men looked identical to each other.

"Why do you keep calling me Marshal? My name is…"

"You are the Marshal of the Eastern Territories because you killed the previous Marshal."

She couldn't believe her ears.

"What are you talking about? I didn't kill anyone."

"Your airship landed on her while she was giving a speech in the town square."

Dorothy lowered her head and shut her eyes tight and tried to control the thoughts spinning in her head. "I didn't mean to kill anyone. I am so sorry."

Munch, or at least she thought it was Munch as he was the only one who did any talking, came forward and put a stubby hand on her knee.

"Don't be. She was as wicked as they come. A real witch with a capital b."

"I don't understand."

"It is customary in OZ that whoever kills the Marshal takes their place."

"So am I the new target for the next yahoo who wants to be Marshal?"

Munch smiled, his three teeth glistening in the light streaming in from the window. "Oh no, you are perfectly safe. Nobody wants to be a Marshal in OZ."

Dorothy stood up and caught her reflection in the mirror. Her mouth gaped open as she looked down at the brown leather corset, leather pants and boots.

"What happened to my clothes?"

"Your clothes were torn and bloody from the crash. Not to mention the fire. It would be indecent for you to walk around as you were. And besides, you're the new Marshal. You had to look like one. It was your good fortune that I was the official tailor for the previous Marshal."

Dorothy felt around her neck. "My emerald! Where is it?"

"What is an emerald?"

"It's small. It's green. It was in a silver necklace."

Munch's brothers all looked at each other and shook their heads. She looked around at all of them. "Where are the clothes I was wearing?"

The little men all looked at the ground. A couple of them blushed.

Munch refused to look her in the eye. "We have no women in the house. We took no liberties, I assure you."

"My clothes. Where are they?"

One of the men pointed to a pile of tattered rags in the corner of the room. She knelt and felt all around, pushing down on the scorched and shredded fabric hoping to hit something solid inside them.

Munch watched her dig through the tattered clothing. "I am sorry; we did not find anything in your clothes."

Dorothy shook her head in total disbelief.

William was dead.

Her necklace was gone.

There was no way she could find her father without it.

She could go back to New Kansas and listen for the radio signal that had sent them here in the first place. Her father had reached out once before and he could do it again. Maybe he would tell them exactly where he was and she wouldn't need the necklace to find him.

"I have to get out of here."

Munch brightened up with the change of subject. "I will show you to your palace."

"I don't mean out of here. I mean out of the Outcast... out of OZ."

"There is no way out of OZ."

"There has to be a way out."

"There is no way out."

She looked around at the small group of men. "Alright. Let's try this a different way. Who is in charge here?"

"You are." One of the men said abruptly.

"No, no. I mean who's in charge here?"

"As long as you wear that shield," Munch pointed to the Marshal shield attached to her leather corset. "You are the law and we will do as you command."

"Then get me out of the... out of OZ."

Munch dropped his shoulders. "There is no way out of OZ."

Another one of Munch's brothers laughed. "Right. Unless you can fly."

That's it, Dorothy thought. The crash cannot have been too bad. Nothing's broken and I'm only slightly scratched up. I can repair the airship and get out here.

She smiled to herself. It paid to be the daughter of a scientist. She'd mastered mechanical engineering skills around the same time most kids were mastering finger painting.

She looked at Munch. "Take me to the airship."

Dorothy stared at the twisted metal, some of it still burning.

The gondola had broken apart into several pieces and was scattered throughout the center of the tiny town.

A leather boot attached to a bloody leg protruded out from under the largest of the gondola fragments.

Munch pointed to the bloody boot and smiled. "Your handiwork."

Dorothy clenched her jaw. "I told you, I did not mean to kill anyone."

Munch nodded. "That is good news indeed. The previous Marshal had no problem killing any of us when the mood struck her."

"I won't be your Marshal for very long. I don't plan on sticking around any longer than I have to."

"We already told you, there is no way out of OZ."

She pointed to the one who spoke earlier. "He said I could get out if I could fly."

"He was joking. The security systems would shoot down any airship that attempted to leave OZ. There is no way out."

"There has to be."

"There isn't."

The other man spoke up. "What about…"

Munch cut him off. "Shh, brother."

Dorothy looked back and forth between Munch and his brother. "What was he going to say?"

Munch walked away from her. "Nothing. He wasn't going to say anything."

She caught back up with him. "He was going to say something until you shut him up."

He stopped. "No. It will not work."

"What won't work?"

He turned to her and looked her in the eyes. "You know why OZ was built, don't you?"

"It is a centralized global prison."

"No. It was built for one man and one man alone. He had escaped from every prison they tried to put him in until they built this place. We are only here because it was cheaper and more agreeable to the human rights activists than killing us outright."

"Kill you? What did you do?"

"That's the thing. I didn't do anything."

"Then why are you in the… in OZ?"

"We are clones."

She looked around at the identical men gathered around her. "Cloning is illegal."

"And so, by proxy, we are illegal. Well, they are anyway. I am the original. They are all clones of me, so technically, I am okay. But it wouldn't do any good to have me running around telling everyone about illegal cloning experiments. So, I was sent here with them."

"How come I never heard about this?"

"This is OZ. It is a one-way trip. They send us here to ease their conscience and then forget about us."

"What about contacting the news media or getting an appeal?"

"There is no contact with the outside. Once you are here…"

"But he was about to tell me something before you shut him up."

"It was a stupid idea."

"Tell me anyway."

He let out a big sigh. "There is someone who seems to be able to contact the outside. If you could get to him, he might be able to get a message to someone that you are here."

"Who is he?"

Munch lowered his head and was quiet for a moment before lifting it again and looking at her. "OZ was created to contain him. He is called the Wizard."

"The Wizard?"

Munch shrugged. "It was a nickname the newspapers gave him because no prison could contain him. You see why it's a stupid idea?"

"Why do you think he can help me?"

"He helps lots of us in OZ. People ask him for favors and he helps them, if they pay his price."

"I don't have any money."

"He never asks for money."

"What's the price?"

"It's different for everyone. Most people, when they find out what he wants in return, give up. He rarely has to do what is asked of him."

"That doesn't sound very fair."

"He's the Wizard. I don't think fair is in his vocabulary."

"What makes you think if he can't get out of OZ, he can help me get out?"

Munch shrugged again. "I told you it was a stupid idea."

Dorothy watched the burning wreckage of the airship in silence for a minute. "But if anyone can help me, he can?"

"I guess."

"Then I will go see this Wizard."

"No. You can stay here and be our Marshal. You have earned that right."

Dorothy looked down at Munch. "I don't belong here."

"Neither do I. But what can you do?"

Dorothy placed her hands on the side of Munch's face. "When I get out, I will tell the world what has happened to you and get you out of here too."

A tear formed in the corners of his eyes. "If you could do that, I would serve you forever."

Dorothy smiled, fighting back her own tears. "Seeing you freed from this place will be enough."

An explosion blew through a wall on the far side of the town square and a massive steam-driven armored carriage with a forward facing carronade, a short smooth-bore cast iron cannon, rolled through the jagged hole it had just created.

Munch's brothers scattered in all directions.

Dorothy grabbed one as he ran by. "What's going on?"

He struggled against her grip. "It's the West Marshal."

She looked at the armored carriage as it rolled to a stop in the middle of the square. "There are other marshals?"

"One for each region." He wriggled free from her grasp and disappeared into the surrounding buildings.

Dorothy stood alone in the town square as she faced the smoking behemoth.

The hatch opened along the top. A woman climbed out and jumped down to the ground.

She stalked over to the wreckage of the gondola and knelt to inspect the bloody boot that poked out from under it.

She stood back up and looked around. Her eyes glossed over Dorothy and kept going as if she wasn't even there. She walked over to a crate lying half broken in the wreckage. She lifted the lid and peered inside. From her vantage point, Dorothy could see that the crate was now empty. Whatever was inside was stolen or possibly destroyed when the airship crashed.

The West Marshal dropped the lid and kicked the crate.

She finally acknowledged Dorothy's existence and walked over to her. She cocked her head to the side and stared at her for a while before finally speaking.

"I take it from that uniform you are the new Marshal?"

Dorothy looked down at her leather corset. "I guess so."

The West Marshal took a long step forward and came face to face with Dorothy, their noses nearly touching.

"Then I guess you are the one who killed my sister."

Chapter 2

Dorothy opened her mouth several times and closed it again, unable to speak.

The West Marshal took a step back and regarded her with a tilt of her head. "What is your name little girl?"

"Dorothy."

"Tell me, Dot, why did you kill my sister?"

"It was an accident. My airship crashed into the... into OZ. I didn't mean to kill anyone. And my name is Dorothy, not Dot."

The West Marshal leaned back in close. Dorothy could smell her rancid breath.

"You, are an insignificant little dot. You are most certainly not worthy of being a Marshal."

"I don't want to be the Marshal."

The West Marshal looked at her in surprise. "You don't?"

"No. I just want to get out of OZ."

The West Marshal smiled sweetly. "I can help you with that."

All the stress of the past few hours melted instantly. "You can?"

"Of course I can. But you have to give me what is rightfully mine."

"I'll give you anything if you get me out."

The West Marshal held out her hand. "The shield. Give it to me."

"The what?"

"The East Marshal shield on your chest."

Dorothy removed the shield attached to the front of her leather corset.

"That's right little girl. Give it to me."

A voice echoed from the doorway of a nearby building. "Don't do it."

The West Marshal hissed at the short figure standing in the doorway. "Stay out of this Munch! You were always trouble for my sister, and yet she let you live. I will not be so forgiving."

Munch ran out and faced the West Marshal. "I am not afraid of you."

The West Marshal laughed. "You should be."

He turned to Dorothy. "Don't do it. OZ was split into four zones to keep any one Marshal from having too much power."

"But she can take me home."

"She will kill you as soon as you give her that shield. She will kill all of us."

"Don't listen to them, Dot. They are all criminals. I am the law."

Dorothy took a step backward. "They are not criminals. And my name is not Dot."

She placed the shield back onto her corset. "It's Dorothy. And as long as I wear this shield, I am the law here."

The West Marshal pointed a sharp finger at her. "You have made the biggest mistake of your life, girly, as short as it will be."

She spun around and stomped back to the armored carriage. She hopped effortlessly to the top of the carriage and looked back at Dorothy. "No little girl playing house with mutants will keep me from what is rightfully mine."

She dropped out of sight and slammed the hatch closed. The carriage spun around on metal covered wheels and disappeared through the hole in the stone wall.

Munch wiped the sweat off his brow. "That went better than expected."

Dorothy spun on her heels to look at him. "How did you expect it to go?"

Munch shrugged again. "We thought she would kill you."

Her mouth gaped open. "You thought…"

"It was a long shot, but it worked. For now."

"What do you mean 'for now'?"

"She will be back and then she will most certainly kill you."

"Oh my God, I have to get out of here. Which way to the Wizard?"

"You will be safer here with us."

"I've tried to be patient with you guys, but I'm not staying."

"If we tell you where to find the Wizard and he cannot help you, will you return and be our Marshal?"

She squeezed her eyes tightly. "Yes. If the Wizard cannot help me, I will come back."

The tiny men all cheered. Dorothy held her arms up to quiet them. "That is a big if."

Munch patted her on the lower back. "Even the faintest glimmer of light can pierce the darkness of the deepest canyon. You have given us a hope that never existed before you freed us from the death-grip of the Marshal before you."

"Great."

"You cannot travel alone. The Woodsmen will surely kill you."

"Woodsmen? What are the Woodsmen?"

"They are judge, jury and executioner for the East Marshal."

"You said that I am the East Marshal."

"They are still following the programmed instructions of your predecessor. Any infraction of the long list of rules will get you put on trial and put to death within seconds of the guilty verdict. They are deadlier than anything else in the Eastern Territories."

Dorothy held up her hands to stop him. "Programmed instructions? You mean the Woodsmen are automatons?"

Munch shrugged his shoulders. "Of course."

"I thought automatons were illegal?"

"Just like me and my brothers, everything illegal is sent here."

She sighed. "Okay, so which of you brave warriors will accompany me on my quest?"

"We have never gone beyond the stone wall. We cannot join you."

"Is this some form of catch 22? I can't travel alone, but none of you will go with me."

"I just meant you need protection. My brother owns an automaton repair shop. He will have exactly what you need."

Dorothy ducked low to get through the doorway into the tiny shop. Munch darted around her and walked up to another clone of himself behind the counter.

"Hey brother."

The little man behind the counter looked up and smiled. "Munch. What brings you here?" He looked past Munch and saw Dorothy. He immediately jumped down from his stool and bowed before her. "My apologies Marshal, I did not see you enter."

Munch lifted the shopkeeper's head. "It is okay. She is our new Marshal."

The shopkeeper's eyes glistened. "It is a wonderful day indeed. What is it you require of me and my humble shop?"

"She is going to see the Wizard."

The shopkeeper looked startled. "No."

"She needs one of your automatons to keep her safe."

"None of my automatons are armed. Most of them are broken and barely work. They could never make the journey to Center City."

"My brother mentioned they brought a new automaton to you this morning."

"He's just a scarecrow."

Dorothy interrupted them. "A what?"

The shopkeeper turned from his brother. He motioned for them to follow as he led them into the back of his shop. He spoke as if giving a tour. "An automaton must be programmed to perform specific tasks. The one they brought in this morning is blank. It only has the basic programming to take verbal instruction and respond to questions."

He stopped in front of a human looking automaton that leaned against the wall with its eyes closed.

The shopkeeper pointed at the automaton. "In this state it is only good for propping up on a stick and scaring the crows out of a field. It can't do anything yet."

Munch stared at the automaton leaning on the wall. "Can it make the journey?"

The shopkeeper took off his glasses and wiped them on his dirty shirt. It seemed to smear the greasy lenses worse than before. "It looks like it was just built, which is most unusual here in OZ. I'm guessing it could make the trip to Center City and back again a hundred times over. But without programming, it still can't do anything."

Dorothy felt her heart pound faster. "Turn it on. Let's see what it can do."

The shopkeeper reached behind the automaton and pushed a pressure panel on its back.

The automaton stood up from against the wall, a faint glow emanating from its amber eyes. "Ready for programming."

The shopkeeper shook his head. "It's like I told you. It cannot do anything yet and I do not have a programming machine. But I'll bet it will make the best darn scarecrow you ever did see."

Dorothy remembered something her father had done once when she was little. She stepped forward and spoke to the automaton. "Initiate adaptive programming."

The automaton's eyes flashed. "Program initiated. Begin instruction."

She turned to Munch. "I can get him anywhere he needs to be just by talking to him. Do you know anyone who can program him with self-defense or hand-to-hand combat?"

Munch shot a look at Dorothy. "Him?"

"I don't feel right about calling him an 'it'."

One of Munch's other brothers spoke up. "They battle with automatons at the coliseum. I bet they could program him."

Munch stared hard at him. He raised his hands in defense. "I heard it from a guy that I trade butter for eggs with on the outside." Munch stared even harder at him. He pointed at Munch. "Don't look at me like that. You love my omelets."

She smiled at Munch's brother. "It sounds like I found a way to program my own protection for the journey." She looked at the automaton. "But first, he needs a name."

The shopkeeper snickered. "How about Scarecrow?"

Dorothy inspected the automaton. "I can't think of anything better. Scarecrow it is."

Scarecrow looked around at the people gathered around him. "My name is Scarecrow."

Dorothy smiled. "That settles it. He can learn."

The shopkeeper looked expectantly at Dorothy. "What do you want to teach him?"

Dorothy looked into the blank stare of the Scarecrow. "He needs to learn how to fight."

Chapter 3

Dorothy climbed the only tower in the walled city that Munch and his clones called home.

Once at the top, she looked out over the wall that surrounded Munch's city and out into OZ itself.

This didn't look like any prison she had envisioned. In fact, looking in every direction into a vast expanse dotted with small towns, rolling hills, forests and the tell-tale signs of larger cities in the distance, this didn't look like a prison at all.

It looked like home. Not specifically her home on the farm, but everywhere she had ever been. Every city she had visited. Every forest she had played in. Everywhere she had traveled looked exactly like what she was looking at now.

Only this was a prison.

She had expected it to look like the vision of a prison in her head. Large cement walls, individual cells for the prisoners, and guards stationed all around to keep the peace.

She never expected it to not look like a prison.

She glanced down at the hole in the wall. Munch's brothers were gathering materials to seal it up as quickly as possible.

What were they so afraid of that they sealed themselves up in a prison within a prison? Not only were they cut off from the outside world by being sent to OZ. They also cut themselves off from the world within OZ.

If I were planning to stay, she thought, I would want to find the answer to that question. But I don't plan to be here for very long.

"A shilling for your thoughts?"

She turned around to see Munch. In the short time she had been there, she could see the slight differences in dress and demeanor between Munch and the rest of his clones.

"What?"

He smiled. His bottom teeth looked yellower in the harsh sun than when she first saw them. "It hardly seemed fair to offer a sixpenny for one of the East Marshal's thoughts."

She turned back to the hole in the wall. "I was just thinking about how much this place looks like anywhere else in the world."

Munch stood next to her and looked out over the horizon. "Most people don't take advantage of the fact that they can travel freely from the place they call home."

He turned back to her. "What about you? What made you travel from your home?"

She didn't look at him and hugged herself tight against the cooling breeze. "I came to New Kansas with my mom and dad. Given everything that's happened, I wish we had stayed in America."

"There, see? Given the choice, you would never have ventured very far from your home. OZ is big enough that we can travel for several days via airship to visit far off lands. All within the confines of the Australis Penal Colony, of course. If you don't think about it too hard, you don't miss the lack of freedom. There's plenty of freedom to go around OZ without having to leave it."

She turned to face him. "Then why the wall?"

He looked out into OZ. "There is still a large element of the criminally insane running around OZ. They are mostly in the Eastern Territories. It looks peaceful out there now…"

His voice trailed off and he remained silent for a few moments before he turned to face her. "Me and my brothers? Let's face it; we would be eaten alive out there. We're not big, we're not strong. I would even go as far to say we're not very brave."

"I saw how you stood up to the West Marshal. That seemed pretty brave to me."

He smiled. "That's because I knew the law would prevent her from doing anything. It seemed a pretty safe thing to do at the time. So no, I'm still not very brave."

They both turned back to stare out over the expanse of OZ for several minutes.

Munch was the first to break the silence. "Are you sure you don't want to stay?"

She half smiled. "I'm sorry, Munch. I have to try and get home so I can find my father."

"In that case I found someone who can take your automaton for combat training."

"You did? See? I knew there was someone brave among you."

"He's from outside the wall. I guess the curiosity of the secrets we keep inside these walls got the better of him. My brothers had him tied up by the time I got there and he was trying to negotiate his release."

"What secrets do you keep in here?"

"None. But since we never leave and nobody ever comes in, he thought we had secrets."

"You said he can help?"

"Before he was discovered, he overheard a couple of my brothers discussing how to teach your automaton how to fight. He promised to take your automaton to the casino and get him trained by the best. He said he knows the man who owns the casino."

She had been in OZ for two days already, and she was further than ever before from finding her father. Every time she took a step, she was forced to take two more steps in the opposite direction. All she wanted to do was get to the Wizard and figure out a way out of OZ. But in order to do that, she had to train scarecrow how to fight just so she wouldn't be killed on her way to Center City.

She had to put her life into the hands of strangers to carry out her goal. And now the strangers had found a new stranger. But if he was willing to help, she would gladly accept it.

"Take me to him."

Dorothy looked into the dark hole in the stone wall. She looked at Munch.

"Why aren't we at a gate?"

"We don't have a gate. Nobody here wants to get out, and we don't want anyone out there getting in. As soon as you leave, we are sealing the hole."

"Where is the man you told me about?"

"He went back through to pack for his journey. He promised to return within the hour."

"And you believed him?"

"What benefit would he receive by lying to me?"

"How about you letting him go?"

"He gave us his assurance he would be back within an hour. I had no reason to doubt him."

She looked at Munch. He was so trusting, even inside the world's largest prison he took people at their word. Maybe it would do him some good to get out of his little secluded haven and meet some real people.

"You sure you don't want to come with me?"

Munch held up his stubby arms. "Look at me. I wouldn't last an hour outside."

Dorothy looked at the little men all standing in the town square. "Your prison within a prison."

Munch smiled. "Such as it is. Ah, here is your escort."

Dorothy looked in to the darkness of the hole. She heard the sound of scuffling feet and watched as a young boy stepped out into the light. She didn't know what to expect, but it wasn't this. "He's just a boy."

The boy looked at Dorothy. "And you're just a girl. Now that we have figured out our genders, how about names? Mine's Jasper."

"Doro…"

Munch interrupted her. "She's the East Marshal. You will be very wise to do as she says."

The boy looked her up and down as if he were appraising a prized cow. "Looks kinda young to be the East Marshal."

She stuck her chin up at him. "You look too young to…" Her voice trailed off, unsure of what to say next. She was never one for the snappy comebacks, and it always put her at a disadvantage back at the farm.

That same easy smile spread across his lips. "Right then. We should get going now if we plan to make it to the casino before dark. As it is, we're cutting it awful close."

Dorothy was still in shock that a boy was in the Outcast Zone. She never heard anything about children being sent to the penal colony. "What did you do to get sent to OZ?"

He shrugged. "Nothing. I was born here."

It was unnerving how nonchalant everyone was. If she ever found herself in the Outcast Zone… What was she thinking? She was in the Outcast Zone.

Jasper pointed at Scarecrow. "That can't go with us."

Dorothy snapped out of her downward spiraling thoughts. "He's why you're here. He has to go with us."

Jasper shook his head. "Nobody said anything about a human form automaton. They are forbidden." He inspected Scarecrow closer. "Looks new. Where did you get it?"

Munch stepped forward. "We found him this morning lying in a field."

"And you didn't wonder where it came from?"

Munch shrugged again. "Things show up all the time inside the wall. We never question our good fortune."

Jasper spun and headed for the hole in the wall. "If that thing is coming along, I can't help you."

Dorothy ran to catch up with him. "He has to come."

He spun back around to face her. "Why?"

She stammered. "I need him for protection."

"What can it do to protect you?"

"Well, nothing yet. That is why you're here. To take him somewhere he can be trained to fight."

He motioned to Scarecrow. "It can't go looking like that. You will need to dress it up. If anyone notices it's not human, we will have more trouble than any of us can handle."

Munch placed the top hat on Scarecrow's head and stepped back to regard his handiwork.

"It looks like a robot pimp," Jasper exclaimed.

Scarecrow, dressed in a floor length brown leather duster, leather gloves and black wig supplemented his look with a long cane that also provided a visual cover for the noise his metallic feet made as he walked.

Munch held his hands out in apology. "It was the only thing I had on hand. The previous Marshal had requested it for a friend of hers."

"Then I guess we know what kind of people she associated with," Jasper remarked.

"But will it work?" Dorothy asked.

Jasper stroked a chin that still had a few years to go before any hair would start growing. "If we cover up those glowing eyes with some goggles, it should pass a quick glance. Nobody really looks too long at anybody else here in OZ. It's a sure sign you want to fight. And you never know what the other guy has up his sleeve."

He glanced at a pocket watch before tucking it back into his vest. "We better get going. Trust me when I say we don't want to find ourselves outside the casino come nightfall."

"I am the East Marshal; doesn't that give me some protection?"

"Not even your predecessor would venture into the gambling district after dark."

"Then why are we going there?"

"You want to teach your automaton to fight, don't you?"

"Of course."

"The arena is the best place to learn."

"I don't have any money. How will I pay for the training?"

Jasper smiled. "I know the owner. I'm sure we can work out some sort of arrangement."

They emerged from the tunnel through Munch's wall. Colorful streamers and confetti filled the street. In the distance, she could hear festive music that was occasionally drowned out by shouting. No, not shouting. More like a large crowd of people cheering.

She followed Jasper through several back alleyways. At the other end of some cross passages, she caught a glimpse of throngs of people dressed up in colorful costumes all dancing in the street.

"Stay close to me. You're lucky to have come during Carnival. It should help us hide you and your automaton's identity better."

"What's Carnival?"

Jasper ignored her question and reached over to tug her cloak closed. "And keep that Marshal star hidden. We don't want anybody seeing who you are or we won't get very far."

She caught up to Jasper and yelled in his ear. "Why are they all dancing?"

"They are dancing for you."

"What do you mean me?"

"Word has spread about the death of the old Marshal and how the new Marshal brought soldiers and weapons to free us from the tyranny of the existing rulers. Munch told me one of your soldiers survived the crash. I know this doesn't say much about the previous Marshal, but the general consensus is relief and excitement. Everyone hopes you will be a better Marshal than the last one."

She wondered how they would all feel if they knew she didn't want the job but was instead trying to get out of OZ as fast as she could.

"I thought you said I arrived during Carnival. This can't all be just for me."

"No, of course not. We celebrate Carnival with the change of the seasons. It is an added bonus that we have a new Marshal."

"You have Carnival four times a year?"

"Yes."

"Is it always this big?"

"This time is bigger than most because of you, but it can still get very big."

"Do any of these people realize they are all in a prison?"

"OZ is only a prison to those on the outside. To us, it is home."

They darted through more back alleys.

"Why are we avoiding the crowds?"

"We would never make it through the city trying to move through the crowds. And if anyone saw you, we wouldn't get anywhere. You are our biggest celebrity. Everyone would want a picture with you."

"You're not going gaga over me?"

"I don't want to be outside the casino when the sun drops below the horizon. I can go gaga over you later."

She didn't know what to think about this boy who was born here and lived his entire life within the confines of the world's largest prison. Of course, nothing she had experienced thus far felt like a prison. It was more like any other city she visited when shopping for new farming equipment with Uncle Henry.

She thought of Uncle Henry and Aunt Em and wondered if they would welcome her back when she got out of OZ.

As they passed an open courtyard area between several buildings, her eye caught the glimpse of tarnished metal and she stopped short. Several young children were climbing on a massive statue. Only it wasn't a statue at all.

Dorothy moved closer and saw that it was a tree cutter automaton. Only now it served as an impromptu play structure for children. Two of them took turns hitting it on the leg with a metal pipe and laughing at the echoing sound that reverberated throughout the armored metal body.

Scarecrow stopped and looked at the rusted automaton with children climbing all over it. Scarecrow stared at it only because she had been staring at it.

Dorothy smiled and pointed to the large machine. "It's a Woodsman model. Now I get it. They re-purposed forest clearing automatons into the local police of OZ."

Jasper ran up to her, out of breath.

"I turned around and you were gone. Why did you stop?"

"Just how dangerous is this city at night?

"Very. If we keep moving we can just make it to the casino."

She regarded the large automaton.

"I want to see if I can get that thing fired up."

"That's been there forever. It doesn't work."

"But if it does, we will be that much safer."

"We don't have time for this."

Dorothy watched the sun dip below the edge of the city skyline in the distance. It would be dark within the hour. "We've already run out of time."

Chapter 4

Dorothy spent the better part of that hour working on the Woodsman. Jasper paced back and forth, muttering to himself while the children gathered around and closely watched her progress.

She wondered if they secretly hoped she couldn't fix it. Otherwise, their playground would, literally, walk away.

Despite the risk of losing their favorite toy, the children were very helpful in collecting tools and even a gallon of oil from the surrounding houses. One of them retrieved some coal for the furnace that powered the Woodsman.

She wanted to believe that they helped because they were curious if she could really fix the Woodsman, but Jasper reminded her that if the Marshal asked for the shirts off their back, they would give them to her.

As long as she wore that shield on her chest, they would obey her.

She tucked in the worn copper wiring, screwed the cover plate closed, and stood back to admire her work.

"Anybody got a match?"

"Yeah," Jasper muttered a little too loudly. "Your face and my butt."

Dorothy shot him a bitter glance.

"Here you are Marshal." One of the little boys, who had taken turns beating the Woodsman with a metal pipe, offered her flint and steel.

She took them and scraped them over the charcloth. The sparks ignited it immediately. She cupped the smoldering cloth in her hands to keep the light breeze from blowing it out and placed it into the Woodsman's firebox.

Everyone took a careful step backward as the firebox began creating the steam that would drive the Woodsman's gears.

There was a loud boom and black smoke engulfed everyone. She gathered the children together and peered through the smoke.

"Is everyone okay?"

She could still hear the huffing sound of the Woodsman's boiler coming from somewhere inside the smoke.

The Woodsman suddenly emerged and everyone reflexively took a step backward as he slowly scanned the group. He focused on two of the boys to her left and approached them. A speaker mounted on the front of the Woodsman crackled and his mechanically modulated voice addressed the group.

"Court is now in session."

She observed the unexpected trial as the Woodsman played back a recorded sound of metal striking metal.

His deep metallic voice echoed throughout the entire courtyard. "The evidence has been presented. How do you plead?"

The two boys knelt in the corner and cried in terror.

"Your plea has been logged. You have been found guilty of attempted destruction of city property and are hereby sentenced to death."

The chainsaws mounted at the end of each of the Woodsman's arms spun to life with a piercing whine.

Dorothy witnessed enough and stepped forward, she wasn't about to let the Woodsman harm these children.

Jasper grabbed her arm. "He'll kill you for interfering."

She stared at his hand.

Jasper released her and held his hand up. "Don't say I didn't warn you."

She moved closer to the Woodsman.

Jasper called out to her. "Can I have your Scarecrow when you are chopped to itty bitty bits?"

She ignored him and stepped in front of the twin spinning chainsaws and stood as tall as she could, but her five foot four frame would never come close to matching the nine and a half feet of welded steel that the Woodsman commanded.

"What do you think you are doing Woodsman?"

The chainsaws continued to spin, but he stopped moving closer.

"I am programmed to uphold the law."

She pointed to the shield on her leather corset. "I am the law here."

"Your shield is a symbol. You are the spirit of the law. I uphold the letter of the law. The two felons behind you have been found guilty of attempted destruction of city property."

She looked around her at the dilapidated and crumbling buildings of this depressed part of the city. How could anyone tell if these kids are destroying anything?

She focused her attention back on the Woodsman. "What destruction?"

"They were beating on me with a metal pipe," said the Woodsman as he stood up straighter, as if filled with a sudden pride. "I am city property."

"How long were you standing there before I repaired you?"

"Two years, nine months, five days, four hours and two minutes."

"They had no idea you were still functioning."

"Ignorance is no excuse."

"They are just kids."

"They are guilty."

"I will not allow you to kill these boys."

"Are you ordering me to commute their sentence?"

"I am asking you to have a heart. Show some empathy for these children."

Dorothy stared at the single unblinking eye of the Woodsman. She tried not to focus on the chainsaws. The sharp blades spinning so close and so fast, the wind they generated wafted at the edges of her hair.

The seconds stretched into minutes while the Woodsman appeared to consider her request. It stood there doing nothing. Nevertheless, nothing was better than anything the Woodsman was capable of doing. She hoped the Marshal shield would keep the Woodsman from cutting her in half.

The chainsaws ground to a stop and the Woodsman lowered his arms.

She let out the breath she wasn't aware she had been holding. It was time to start making some changes around here, and as the new Marshal, that job seemed to fall on her.

She looked up at the nine and a half foot tall behemoth and smiled.

"I am changing your primary function, Woodsman."

Dorothy watched from the shadows as Jasper talked to a man who held his shotgun casually against one shoulder. He obviously did not consider Jasper a threat. It seemed odd that an armed guard stood in front of the rusted door of an abandoned warehouse. Then again, Dorothy was moving around inside the world's largest prison. These people probably hung onto every piece of scrap as if it were pure gold.

Jasper finished and ran back across the street to meet up with Dorothy.

"He said for a hundred, we can spend the night inside."

"I don't have any money."

"Don't look at me, I'm twelve."

Dorothy stared across the street.

She started to cross the street. Jasper caught her arm and stopped her. "What are you doing?"

"You keep telling me it's not safe out here at night."

"It's not."

"We need to get inside somewhere now, right?"

He let her arm go and followed behind as she approached the man standing in front of the door.

He was much taller up close than she expected.

He stepped forward and put a hand up.

"I already told your friend, no money, no room."

She smiled her warmest smile. "I'm afraid I am new around here and am not familiar with your customs. I don't even really belong here."

The guard laughed. "None of us do missy. But the world decided it was better to forget about us than to deal with us."

"I'm just looking for a place to spend the night."

"Then you best keep looking. As soon as that sky gets a shade darker, I'm going to be on the other side of that door and won't be responsible for what happens out here."

Dorothy looked around at the deserted street. She had spent several hours in OZ outside of Munch's compound, and so far, everyone behaved like people in any city.

She turned back to the guard. "Everyone keeps talking about how dangerous this place becomes when the sun goes down. What happens?"

The guard leaned in close as if to disclose some big secret. "That's when the people who deserve to be in here come out to play."

The guard stepped back to the door and knocked twice. "It's been fun chatting with you, but my dinner is getting cold."

The door opened and he started inside.

Dorothy stepped up the first step. The guard spun around, racked his shotgun and pointed it at her.

"Stay back missy. Don't make me do something I'm just going to have to clean up in the morning."

"Eckert!" A woman emerged from the open door. "What are you doing?"

Eckert immediately lowered the shotgun and bowed slightly to the woman.

"My job ma'am."

"Your job is not to turn away strangers when the sun has already gone down."

She turned to Dorothy and opened the door wider. "You will have to excuse him. Manners are not something that comes naturally in OZ. Please, come inside."

Dorothy and Jasper followed her into the warehouse. Eckert locked the door from the inside and joined them in the abandoned warehouse.

Dorothy fell alongside the woman as they walked. "I don't mean to be any trouble."

The woman laughed. It was the first genuine laugh Dorothy had heard since crashing in the Outcast Zone. "It's no trouble at all. Eckert's best quality is his ability to follow orders without question. It is what got him sent here in the first place. He listened to the wrong people. Fortunately, he found his way to us before he could get into any more trouble. A lot like the two of you. My name is Mary."

"I'm Dor…"

Jasper interrupted her before she could finish. "She's the new East Marshal."

Mary glanced sideways at her as they continued to walk through the empty warehouse. "I gathered that from the star poking its way out of her cloak."

Dorothy pinched her cloak closed with one hand as if ashamed of her new-found status in OZ.

Mary stopped in the middle of the warehouse at a cast iron grate in the floor. Eckert grabbed one side of the grate and lifted. It swung upward to reveal stairs leading down. The stench from below overpowered Dorothy's senses. She stumbled back as if physically hit. How could people live under such conditions?

Mary looked down the hole. "Home sweet home."

Dorothy followed Mary to the bottom of the stairs. Her eyes adjusted to the darkness as they descended and she saw the rotting animal carcasses nailed to the wall.

Once at the bottom, Mary retrieved an oil lamp from its hook. They were at the end of a long tunnel that faded off into blackness beyond the weak reach of Mary's lamp. She heard Eckert shut and lock the grate above them. It sealed in the smell of death and despair. She had to suppress the overwhelming urge to vomit.

Despite Mary's warm smile and easy manner, Dorothy could not help but feel trapped. OZ was more than just a prison. It was a prison, inside a prison, inside another prison. Mary moved on ahead and turned the corner. Her light faded quickly.

Jasper and Dorothy looked at each other. He shrugged his shoulders and took his hand away from his mouth momentarily. "If they planned to eat us, they would have killed us outside."

Eckert arrived at the bottom of the stairs. "What are you waiting for?"

He shouldered past them and disappeared around the dark corner.

Jasper glanced at her and grimaced. "I hate the dark."

He followed Eckert around the corner leaving her alone at the base of the stairs.

She suddenly wished she had brought Scarecrow with her. Even though he couldn't do anything but follow her like a little lost puppy, just having him by her side would make someone think twice before doing anything.

No, she thought. Jasper was right. If anyone knew she had, not one, but two automatons in her possession, they would be used as currency to get food or a place to sleep for the night. Still she was uneasy about ordering them to stay put, covered in garbage in some back alley, until she returned.

They had not complained, but they deserved better.

Before all the light from Mary's lamp faded away completely, Dorothy rushed to catch up.

The tunnel was composed of several turns, but no branches. There was no risk of getting lost down here. There was only one way to go. At the second turn, she heard the sound of rushing air. She looked up and saw a massive turbine pulling the foul smelling air up and out of the tunnel. Just past the turbine, someone placed orange peels into mesh bags and hung them on the walls. The fragrant fruit, along with the turbine, eliminated the stench from the rotting flesh at the start of the tunnel. From this spot deep underground, OZ smelled better than ever. It even smelled better than Aunt Em's farm in the springtime when everything was in bloom.

She heard the murmur of a multitude of voices talking over one another from around the corner and walked faster. She rounded the next corner and could see light up ahead at the next corner; the murmur of voices grew louder with each step.

She rounded the final corner and her mouth fell open at the sight before her.

The ceiling of the chamber that the tunnel emptied into stood fifty feet above them. The entire ten thousand square foot hollowed out space was well lit. Rows of tables lined the center of the chamber where at least a hundred people were all sitting, laughing, talking, and eating.

Dorothy's stomach growled. She hadn't realized how hungry she was until the savory smells from the feast wafted toward her from the long tables.

Mary came up to her with a young girl at her side. "I'd like you to meet Mara, my daughter. She will show you where you can get cleaned up for dinner."

Jasper called out to her from one of the tables where he had already piled food onto a plate in front of him. "This sure beats the half cooked rat tail I usually get at home." Barbecue sauce ran down the sides of his mouth and dripped off his chin as he tore another chunk of rabbit meat from the bone and popped it into his mouth.

Mara took her over to a small basin filled with warm water and demonstrated washing her hands, which Dorothy did several times, before wiping them on a clean towel. Dorothy looked around at the families gathered together laughing and eating as Mara led her back to the table with Jasper and her mother. As Dorothy sat down, she leaned over to Mara. "What is this place?"

"This is the fellowship room. We come here to celebrate the day's bounty."

"Is this part of Carnival?"

"We do not participate in Carnival. It is not permitted by the Doctrine of Wisdom."

Dorothy furrowed her eyebrows. "I'm sorry, the what?"

"The Doctrine of Wisdom. The Prophet of OZ gave it to us to help us avoid the bad things in life."

Mary leaned over Mara. "Please forgive my daughter. She rarely meets anyone from outside Chambers. What my daughter means is…"

Mara's eyes lit up as she cut off whatever her mother was about to say. "The Doctrine tells of an outsider who will rescue us from this horrible place. We received word that a warrior has fallen from the sky and slain the wicked Marshal.

Tonight is a special dinner. We are celebrating the arrival of our savior."

Mary's brow furrowed. "Mara, hush. Do not bother our guest with bedtime stories."

Mara's eyes sparkled as she peered deeply into Dorothy's eyes. "Are you here to save us?"

"That is enough Mara. You may be excused."

"But Mom…"

"Get ready for bed."

"Abigail's mom is letting her stay up for the dance."

"Mara," she hissed.

Mara pushed her plate back and stomped away from the table.

Mary watched her go before turning to Dorothy. She folded her napkin into her lap and stared at Dorothy with a nervous smile. "Please excuse my daughter. She has quite the imagination."

"Is this doctrine a religion?"

"Don't be silly. Religion is illegal in OZ. It is merely the principles by which we govern ourselves."

Music swelled on the far side of the massive underground cavern. Mary looked over Dorothy's shoulder and a wave of relief washed over her face. "The dance is about to begin, please feel free to join us." Mary stood up quickly and left the table.

Jasper snatched a small roasted potato off his plate and stuffed it into his mouth. He chewed it while he spoke. "I've heard about Chambers. Some hidden city beneath OZ where you can pray if you want to. The folks down here are all nut jobs." He popped another potato into his mouth. "But they sure do know how to cook."

Dorothy watched the dancing from the sidelines. She couldn't believe that people could have so much fun while living in a prison. A few times, someone would sway and undulate over to her and try to coax her out onto the dance floor. She refused each time as politely as she could.

As her most recent dance suitor spun back into the throng of bodies, Eckert walked up and sat down next to her.

He nodded his head at the dancers moving in a slow circle like a school of fish. "You don't dance?"

"Nope. Never was any good at it."

"Me neither."

They sat in silence and watched the crowd. He said something so softly that Dorothy didn't quite hear him the first time. "What was that?"

Eckert half turned toward her and spoke louder. "What are your intentions?"

"I have no intentions. I just need a place to stay tonight. You know, away from whatever nightmare is going on outside."

"They are good people. They took me in when I was at my lowest. I would do anything to protect them." He turned to face her directly. "Anything."

She didn't know how to respond. They silently stared at one another, neither saying a word for nearly a minute. Eckert suddenly smiled. "I'm glad we had this talk."

He stood up and waded through the dancing crowd.

As she watched the bodies sway and move to the rhythm provided by the drums, she reached to fiddle with her emerald necklace. It was something she often did out of habit while thinking. Her hand searched her neck in vain before she consciously remembered losing it in the crash and folded her hands in her lap.

She thought back on her own life and how unfair it seemed. Her mother dead. Her father missing. All of that paled in comparison to these people who were forced to live underground in OZ.

Yet, they seemed to be happy.

Not just faking it, but really happy.

Someone bumped into her as they sat down. She looked down as Mara looped an arm through hers and snuggled close. "Mother says I'm too young to dance, but I can watch."

Dorothy smiled at her. "Your mother seems like a very nice person."

"She is, for the most part. Other times, she acts like a mother." She looked up at Dorothy. "Is your mother nice?"

Dorothy looked out into the circle of dancers. "Yes, she was very nice."

Mara must have picked up that she referred to her mother in the past tense and squeezed her arm softly. "You should move to Chambers. We are safe here from the dangers outside."

She didn't know how to tell this little girl that she grew up outside of OZ. How could she begin to explain that life outside of OZ was not as dangerous as it was inside when her own mother died violently in one of the safest cities in the Southern Hemisphere?

She decided it was best not to say anything as she stifled a yawn. "I should be getting some sleep."

"Will I see you in the morning?"

"I plan to leave very early."

"Breakfast usually starts before the sun rises." She looked at the dancers. "My guess is it will start even before that."

"I will ask if you are awake before I leave. If you are, we can say goodbye."

"I'd like that," Mara said and pointed to a thick curtain that hung over an opening. "You can find a soft bed in the sleep chamber through there."

"How will I know which bed to use?"

"Nobody owns anything in Chambers. You can just pick the first empty bed you find."

Dorothy stood and made her way to the curtain Mara had pointed out.

On the other side of the curtain was another large chamber filled with beds.

Each bed had privacy curtains attached to the six-foot tall bedposts. Even though everyone slept in the same room, they all had a private place to sleep.

She found an empty bed near the entrance and pulled the privacy curtains closed. They did a good job of blocking out most of the subdued lighting of the sleep chamber, but nothing could muffle the noise still echoing down the hallway from the fellowship chamber. The musicians took occasional breaks, but had informed everyone they would be playing until the sun came up.

I guess it's better than whatever was going on outside, Dorothy tried to reassure herself.

She settled into the soft bed and closed her eyes.

She was exhausted.

The last twenty-four hours had proven to eclipse anything in her life that came before. The airship crash. Walking half the day through OZ, and she still didn't think she had really managed to get very far. She had heard stories of how big this place was, but it didn't really hit home until she walked its streets on foot.

Dorothy drifted off to a dreamless sleep.

She woke instantly when something cut off her air supply. She nearly screamed in surprise but Eckert looked sternly at her with his hand still clamped tightly over her mouth.

Eckert put a finger to his lips. "Shh."

Dorothy nodded that she understood.

He pulled his hand away from her mouth.

She whispered. "What's going on?"

"Somebody's looking for you."

She rubbed the sleep from her eyes.

"Who?"

"She didn't give a name, but she doesn't look like a friend. Mary is stalling her while I sneak you out the back. It's almost morning and you can travel outside."

"What does she look like?"

"Black cloak. Brown hair. You know her?"

She mentally scrolled through the short list of people she had met after the crash and shook her head. "No."

"We have to go quietly."

Dorothy sat up. "I want to see her."

"Follow me... What?"

"I want to meet with her."

"Mary doesn't trust this woman. She told me to get you out of here."

"No. I can end this. I am the East Marshal after all."

Eckert clearly did not know what to do. He was great at following orders, but Dorothy just gave him conflicting orders. He searched her face for some sign that she would follow him out of Chambers. When he didn't see any, his shoulders dropped as he let out a sigh. "If I take you to see this woman, will you tell Mary that I tried to get you out?"

"Of course. You are doing the right thing. You'll see."

She followed him through several tunnels. She could hear voices as they approached another chamber entrance. One of the voices was Mary, and the other was the voice of a young woman. "I assure you, I will not tell anyone how to find the entrance to Chambers when I leave. As long as I get what I came for."

"I'm not sure how we can help you. As I have already informed you, Amanda was it?"

Amanda nodded her head and Mary continued. "The Marshal left early this morning…"

Mary was shocked to silence when Eckert stepped aside to let Dorothy in to Study Chambers. The young woman, who Mary had referred to as Amanda, looked at Dorothy as she came in the room and her eyes darkened.

Dorothy smiled at her despite the obvious hostility. "I came back when I heard someone was looking for me. Now, what is so important that I had to return?"

Amanda stood up from her chair. "The West Marshal sent me to collect what belongs to her."

Dorothy's hand reached for the Marshal star pinned to her chest and touched it lightly. She looked back up at Amanda. "According to the laws of this land, it belongs to me."

"You are an outsider. You do not deserve to join the ruling family."

"What ruling family?"

"Both the east and west regions of OZ were joined by blood. My mother and her sister were the marshals of both. I was next in line to inherit them. Not an outsider."

"I thought you could only inherit a Marshal's star by killing them?"

"Or by gift. When my aunt got too old, she was to give the East Marshal star to me."

"I'm sorry to have ruined your plans."

Amanda held out her hand. "You will give me my star."

Dorothy took a step backward and covered the star with her hand. "I'm afraid I can't do that."

Amanda dropped her head and studied the ground for a moment. She looked back up, as she removed a device, no bigger than a matchbox, from her cloak pocket. Her thumb hovered just above the single red button. "Have it your way."

Amanda pushed the button.

Dorothy tensed for an explosion to rock Chambers.

Amanda smiled and raised the device to her lips.

"Shut them down."

Dorothy never noticed the constant hum of the turbines that fed fresh air into the underground caverns until they powered down and stopped completely. The silence was deafening.

Eckert made a move toward Amanda. Her other hand appeared from inside her cloak holding a revolver and she pointed it at him. He stopped in his tracks and looked to Mary for guidance.

Mary looked at Amanda. "You can't shoot everyone here."

"We both want something. You want air for your families," Amanda motioned toward Dorothy with the gun. "I want what she took from me."

Mary stared unblinking at Amanda. "I will not allow bloodshed to defile Chambers. Take her out of here and leave us in peace." She looked at Dorothy. "I am very sorry. I have over forty families to look after down here. We have enough troubles of our own and can't afford to take yours on as well."

Dorothy took a deep breath. "I understand."

"I am truly sorry." She looked at Eckert. "Please take our guest," she glanced sideways at Amanda. "And her friend back to the surface. Once they are outside the compound, get some men to see how much damage was done to the turbines."

"Yes ma'am."

Amanda lowered her revolver but did not take her eyes off Eckert. "You might want to bring some spare electrical cable and welding equipment. My men will help with the repairs."

Mary nodded her head. "That is most generous of you."

Amanda smiled. "You have been very accommodating. It's the least I can do."

Mara pushed on the thin wire mesh grate. It gave way and fell to the ground. She hopped down and out of sight.

Jasper wriggled forward on his belly and looked out the opening she had just made. They were only a couple feet from the ground. He hopped down after her.

"What are we doing out here?"

"My mom used the phrase."

"What phrase?"

"Any time she says that we can't take on someone else's problems, that is exactly what she wants us to do."

He looked around at the empty warehouse. "When do the others get here?"

She looked at him quizzically. "What others?"

"The people who will be joining us to rescue the Marshal."

She laughed. "We're not meeting anyone. We are the only ones who can help your friend."

"You're crazy. We don't even know how many men that maniac has up here. What can we do?"

"I saw the automaton you hid in the alley. The big one with the chainsaws. When they come out of Chambers, we can use it to rescue your friend."

Jasper looked at Mara with a new sense of respect. "Why didn't I think of that?"

They ran across the street and down the alley where the Woodsman and Scarecrow stood waiting.

They pulled the garbage off the Woodsman and looked up at him.

Jasper stared at the unblinking eye. "Hey, you."

He stood stock-still and didn't respond.

"Hey. Come with me."

He didn't move or react to Jasper who started jumping up and down more wildly.

"Yo. Idiot. I order you to follow me."

The Woodsman remained perfectly still. Mara ran to the corner and peeked around it. She ran back to Jasper. "They're just coming out of the warehouse. Maybe we need to think of something else."

Jasper looked around him and spotted what he was looking for. "We haven't tried everything yet."

He picked up a long metal pipe. "Get ready to run."

Amanda shoved Dorothy ahead of her out the door of the warehouse and onto the street. The sun peeked over the edge of the city skyline in the distance.

Amanda turned back toward Eckert. "My men can also repair the damage to the grate."

He looked at her, no emotion on his face. "Don't bother. We will be sealing up that entrance."

Eckert looked sad as he swung the door closed and Dorothy heard the lock click.

Amanda pointed her revolver at her. "I could kill you right now and take the star."

Dorothy lifted her chin in defiance. "You're going to have to, because I need it."

Amanda's eyes burned with hatred. She grabbing Dorothy by the neck and slammed her into the wall. She shoved the revolver in her face. "Give it to me now!"

Before Dorothy could respond, they both heard the loud crashing of metal. Jasper darted around the corner of the warehouse with Mara hot on his heels. A familiar metallic voice echoed from the alley they had just run from. "If you continue to run, evading arrest will be added to your guilty sentence."

The Woodsman rounded the corner in pursuit of the two children. He stopped as his single eye focused on Amanda holding a gun to Dorothy.

"You are guilty of unauthorized possession of a firearm with intent to harm a Marshal. The sentence for this crime is death. Please remain still while I carry out your sentence."

The Woodsman's chainsaws whined to a fast blur.

Amanda turned the gun on the Woodsman and fired. The Woodsman moved toward her as the bullets pinged off his metal shell.

Amanda kept firing until she ran out of bullets.

"The crime of attempted destruction of city property has been added to your sentence."

Amanda backed into the corner with nowhere to run. The Woodsman raised his arms, as he got closer. She knelt down on the ground and cried out.

Dorothy yelled, "As Marshal, I grant her a full pardon of all crimes."

The Woodsman stopped and powered down the chainsaws.

Amanda stood up and dusted herself off. "Don't think that by sparing my life that this is over."

Amanda stepped around the Woodsman, keeping a close eye on the chainsaws before she turned and ran off.

The Woodsman's eye rotated to watch her disappear around the corner. It rotated back to look at Dorothy. "Do you want me to pursue her?"

"No, Woodsman. Let her go."

"Based on her language, she is still a threat."

Dorothy smiled up at the Woodsman.

"That is why I have you to protect me."

Scarecrow walked up to them. "What about me?"

"We still need to teach you how to fight."

She looked around for Jasper and Mara, but they were gone.

"Jasper," she called.

Jasper and Mara popped up from behind a trash can and ran over.

"Thank you both for saving me."

The Woodsman spun up his chainsaws. Dorothy turned to him. "They are also pardoned."

The Woodsman lowered his chainsaws. If an automaton could look dejected, he did.

Mara spoke up. "My mother wishes to apologize for making you think she was abandoning you."

Dorothy smiled down at Mara. "Tell your mother I am grateful for everything she did for me. I hope someday I can repay her."

Mara ran off and Dorothy looked at Jasper.

"How long before we can get to this casino of yours?"

He smiled. "We can be there in a couple hours."

Chapter 5

Dorothy followed Jasper as he took them through various enclaves where people gathered for protection. She felt like she had stepped back in time to feudal Europe where people walled themselves inside castles to protect them from their neighbors.

These people had so little compared to what she was used to, even in the farming community of New Kansas. Yet they fought hard to protect what they had.

She could not blame them. The prerequisite for living here was that you could not live peacefully in civilized society.

At least that was supposed to be the prerequisite. Now family groups were forming and children were being born. OZ was becoming an organized society whether the politicians in the outside world liked it or not.

When she got out of here, she would find a way to tell the world what she found. OZ was no longer the prison everyone believed it to be.

Jasper paused at the top of a hill. She caught up to him and stared into the valley below. She gawked in amazement. She wasn't in feudal Europe anymore. She had just stepped back even farther to the height of the Roman Empire.

Spread out before her was a sprawling metropolis of Greek architecture. Every building and structure was carved from white marble. After seeing the multi-colored patchwork of Munch's place, the colorful decorations of Carnival, even the blending of supposedly conflicting styles in Chambers, it was odd to see all color absent from the scenery. Every building was a blank white canvas.

"What is all this?"

Jasper pointed down to the largest building with hundred foot columns all around it supporting the roof. "That is the casino. The city grew up around it and followed the same style."

"Why Greek?"

"It was the inspiration for the arena."

"What arena?"

Jasper pointed to the other side of the valley at an exact replica of the Roman Colosseum. At least it looked like an exact replica. Dorothy barely remembered the time before she ended up on the farm. And to be honest, she never made it successfully out of New Kansas until the fateful airship crash. She never traveled the world to see anything left behind by past civilizations. But she had seen the scratchy and overexposed photographs taken by her father on his adventures when he was younger.

"Is that the place where they can program Scarecrow?"

"Yep."

"Let's get him down there, train him and then head for the Wizard."

"Yes ma'am. I'll let him know you are coming." Jasper ran off.

"Let who know?"

Jasper was already running full speed down the hillside and most likely never heard her. If he had, he didn't bother to stop and answer.

She turned toward Scarecrow. "Scarecrow, come with me. Woodsman, you stay here and…"

"Negative. As long as there is a credible threat on your life, I will stay by your side."

She sighed heavily and started down the hill. "Come on then. And try to blend in."

Scarecrow looked up at the nine and a half foot tall death machine and said, "Would you like to borrow my hat?"

Dorothy walked through the center of the whitewashed city. It felt strange to see a city in OZ that wasn't covered under a layer of dirt and grime. Beyond that, the city didn't look like it had evolved gradually in stages like the other places she had walked through. This city looked planned.

It shattered every preconceived notion she ever had of the Outcast Zone.

Her next thought hit like a thunderbolt. The only difference between those inside OZ and those outside was one group was forced to live where they were, and the other had no choice.

How was she any different from those here in OZ?

There was one way she was different.

She didn't belong here.

She let the press of people move around her as she entered the main street that led to the massive casino.

Booths were scattered on both sides of the street where the owners promoted their wares, shoving whatever it was they were selling right into her face.

"Fresh fish for five. Three for ten."

She winced. "Doesn't smell very fresh."

"Well excuse me, your highness. It doesn't get any fresher than…"

The Woodsman had stopped right behind Dorothy. The fish monger stared up at him and then back to Dorothy. "You must be a gladiator. I wondered about the leather outfit. You will need something to keep your strength up." He shoved the fish into her face again.

"No thanks."

The man frowned. "Then move along. Your toy is scaring away my real customers."

Dorothy noticed that as soon as the Woodsman got closer to her, the constant press of bodies she waded through in the street market dissipated. Nobody wanted to get too close to those chainsaw blades, spinning or not. She didn't blame them. She often found herself looking at them and wondering whether the reddish stains between the teeth of the blades were rust or blood.

A large man with a rifle strapped to his back stepped right in front of her. "Are you the East Marshal?"

The Woodsman noted the rifle, moved in front of Dorothy, and raised his chainsaws. Dorothy placed a hand on the Woodsman's arm. "Hold up." She pulled her cloak to one side, exposing the star pinned to her chest. "Let's hear what he has to say."

The man looked the Woodsman up and down before proceeding. "I am under orders to take you and your automatons to the casino."

"I think we can find it on our own."

"It was not a request."

"It's the largest building at the end of this street. I can see it clearly from here."

"I must insist."

She stared into his eyes and saw nothing but empty blackness. "If I refuse?"

Several more men with rifles stepped out of the crowd and surrounded them. The Woodsman spun up his chainsaws and prepared to defend her, despite being surrounded.

Dorothy did not try to stop the Woodsman this time and looked at the man. "I don't think shooting me is in keeping with the spirit of your orders."

After a short pause, he lowered his rifle. The rest of the men followed his lead and lowered their rifles as well.

The attempt of a smile spread across his pockmarked face. "Will you... please... come with me?"

Dorothy smiled. "Since you asked so politely."

The Woodsman lowered his arms and shut down the chainsaws.

The man walked ahead and the crowd parted out of his way without him saying a word.

The white marble casino towered overhead as she got closer. Dorothy's mind spun back to when the West Marshal called her an insignificant little dot.

Never before had she felt so small. She had traveled to large cities with Uncle Henry a few times and gawked at the massive structures like every hick from the county did.

But this was entirely different.

This single building put everything she had ever seen before to shame.

And it was inside the Outcast Zone.

Inside a prison.

"Keep moving ma'am."

She looked at the guard. "What's the hurry?"

The guard stared straight ahead as he walked. "Just following orders ma'am."

"Can we follow them a little more slowly?"

She slowed down, fell alongside Scarecrow and whispered to him. "What do you make of all this Scarecrow?"

He whispered back. "I don't make anything of it."

"You've been observing quietly for quite some time now. Surely, you noticed something."

"I have no frame of reference to base my observations on."

"So, as far as you are concerned, everything is normal."

"I have no preconceived basis for normal."

"I am supposed to be the East Marshal. The person in charge around here. But every time I turn around, someone else is telling me what to do."

"Maybe if you were a little more assertive people would respect your authority."

She let a wry smile form on her lips. "How is it that someone with two very capable automatons protecting her can't seem to do what she wants?"

"Without programming, I am not as capable as you think. And every time the Woodsman tries to protect you, you stop him."

"So, you have been observing?"

"And learning. Currently I know how to walk all day, how to stop the Woodsman from cutting people in half, and how to get into trouble with just about everyone we meet."

She smiled. "You've also learned how to be a smart ass."

Far above Dorothy, Scarecrow, and the Woodsman, in a tall marble tower overlooking the city that he built around his casino, stood Nero.

That wasn't his given name at birth. Nobody inside OZ knew his birth name; and he planned to keep it that way.

Nero Claudius Caesar Augustus Germanicus was a psychopath and had made many mistakes when he was Emperor over Rome nearly 2,000 years prior. Nero was not a psychopath and would not make the same mistakes when he united all of OZ. He would not sit idly by and watch his city burn like his namesake.

A faint chime sounded above the only door to the room. "Come."

He turned away from the window as the door opened to his private study.

A woman dressed in a black flowing cloak brushed past Caleb, his personal bodyguard, and strode in as if she owned the place.

He decided to forgive her arrogance and smiled at her. "Amanda. It is nice to finally meet you face to face. Your mother says great things about you. Caleb, offer the young lady a glass of water."

She looked him in the eye and did not smile back. "I'm not thirsty. Tell me you have her."

He raised his eyebrows in surprise but decided to let her think she was in charge. At least for a little while.

He needed her.

More to the point, he needed access to her mother.

Her mother had not ventured out of her fortress in over a decade for fear that someone would attempt to assassinate her. Not an entirely unfounded fear, he reminded himself. Yet, she had left the safety of her empire and ventured in to the Eastern Territories to make direct contact with the girl who had taken over as the new East Marshal.

Why was she not afraid of the girl who had killed her sister?

She had returned to her fortress in the West before news traveled throughout OZ that she had even left. News travels fast in Oz, if it was any indication of how quick her trip must have been.

Now she was sending out her daughter to finish what she started.

She obviously decided the new East Marshal was of no threat to her. Moreover, this little tidbit of information was extremely useful to him.

Amanda placed balled fists on her hips and did her best to stare him down. "Well?!"

"She is in custody and being brought to me."

"You were instructed to deliver her straight to me."

"I changed my mind."

"Don't toy with me, Nero."

"I'm not toying with you, my dear."

"Then why haven't you done as you were commanded?"

"Because there are some things you have no control over. When you step foot in my casino, I am the law. I am everything."

"This is not…"

He held a hand up and silenced her. "You will get what you came for. You will get it when I say. I need to make sure that she's not a threat."

"She's not a threat to you or to anybody."

"Then why do you want her so bad?"

"I want to present her to my mother."

"That won't be necessary."

"You promised to turn her over to me!"

"I promised her to your mother. And your mother will have her when she arrives."

"My mother is coming here?"

He smiled. "Your mother's about to become the most powerful Marshal in all of OZ. I should think your time would be better spent finding out her travel itinerary rather than harassing me."

Amanda spun around and stormed out of the room. Caleb closed the doors behind her.

Nero stared at the closed doors for a moment and then looked at his bodyguard.

"What do you think about her, Caleb?"

"I wouldn't know, sir."

"Oh come now, you were created from spliced lion and human DNA. You have the best of both worlds. If your intellect doesn't tell you anything, what does your instinct have to say?"

"She appears to have her own agenda. That might put her loyalty into question, sir."

"That is the impression I got. But then again, nobody will ever be as loyal to me as you."

"You saved me from the fate of my people."

"Yes, I did, didn't I?" His eyes glazed over as he focused on the past. "The outsiders dumped your entire freak show into OZ. The locals decided you were too much animal and not enough human. By the time I heard what was happening…" His face contorted from the memory. "I was too late. When I arrived with my troops… I ordered them to fire on the bastard who was beating a woman to death while she protected a tiny baby in her arms. She lived long enough to make me promise to care for him as if he were my own son."

He looked at the lion-like characteristics of his personal bodyguard. "Now you are all grown up and protecting me."

Caleb bowed his furry head. "I would die for you Father."

He smiled. "You are all too human, Caleb."

Caleb's teeth glistened when he smiled. "Thank you, sir."

Dorothy stared up at the massive door that stood over twenty feet tall and loomed above her head like a doorway for giants. Who could afford this kind of extravagance in OZ?

The doors stood permanently open and people traveled in a constant stream in and out of the casino lobby, like ants entering and exiting an ant colony. Everyone rushed about not worrying about what anyone else was doing.

Each doing the bidding of the Queen of the colony.

Out of the corner of her eye, she thought she saw Scarecrow shiver. She took a deep breath and let it out slowly. "I know. I've got a bad feeling about this too."

The guard stopped under the open archway and turned back toward her. He looked past her and nodded. She followed his gaze and turned around as the other guards withdrew long poles from under their cloaks.

The poles crackled with electricity as they touched them to Scarecrow and the Woodsman. Both automatons instantly shut down. Scarecrow landed on his back with a heavy thud while the Woodsman remained standing, but did not move.

She spun back around to the guard who now held a pole of his own.

"What the…"

Dorothy never had the chance to finish her statement before the end of the pole jabbed into her stomach and a surge of electricity coursed through her body. Her mouth filled with the sour metallic flavor of blood and everything went black.

Dorothy slowly became aware of the soft bed that supported her and the warm covers that swaddled her. She also became aware of the tender spot on her tongue that she bit when they electrocuted her.

Her eyes fluttered open and slammed shut against the sudden rush of light.

"Oh good, you're awake."

She opened them slower this time and focused on the young girl who stood at the foot of the bed. Had she been standing there the whole time waiting for Dorothy to wake up?

She looked at the girl who could not be any more than 10 or 11 years old. Her porcelain skin practically glowed and her braided hair fell half way down her back in golden strands. A stark contrast from the grungy and unkempt hair of the other children she had met the past couple of days in OZ.

When Dorothy got out, she would do something about the conditions these children were forced to live in. They were not in OZ because of anything they had done. No one outside of the Outcast Zone even mentioned that children were being born here.

She looked around her. The room was richly decorated, but she wasn't looking for anything materialistic. She was looking for a whom.

She turned back to the young girl. "Where's Jasper?"

The girl looked puzzled for a moment and then answered. "Oh. The boy who heralded your arrival. He received his reward and departed."

"Reward? Reward for what?"

There was that blank stare again for a moment before the girl responded. "He supplied two new automatons for the games."

"Two automatons? He didn't have any…"

It suddenly dawned on her that Jasper had betrayed her. She silently cursed herself for not seeing it sooner. But then again what could she expect from someone who was born and raised in a prison?

Dorothy shot up in bed and instantly regretted it. Her stomach cramped where the electric baton had zapped her.

The girl was instantly at the side of the bed. "You have to stay in bed. You must rest."

She winced and pulled away the covers of the bed. "I don't have to do anything."

She tried to stand up but the girl placed a hand on her chest and pushed her back onto the bed. The girl slowly forced her into a prone position and held her effortlessly against the bed with one hand as she pulled up the covers with the other.

The girl wasn't hurting her, but Dorothy couldn't move.

"What are you?"

"I am your chambermaid."

"You're not... human."

The girl cocked her head in a human-like gesture. "Do I need to be?"

"Where am I?"

The doors opened up and a man, dressed in a white tuxedo with pink bow tie, strode into the room. He smiled at Dorothy. "Welcome to Casino Roma. The best casino in all of OZ."

She could not believe what she was seeing. "Who are you?"

"My name is Nero and I am at your service," he bowed slightly. "I must say how honored I am to have such a distinguished, and important, guest staying in my casino tonight."

Dorothy regarded the hand that still held her down. "More like a prisoner."

"Don't be silly. Prisoners don't get a private chambermaid."

"Do you think she could let me go?"

Nero thought for a moment. "Alice, you may let our guest up now."

Alice released Dorothy and stepped back.

Dorothy tossed the covers aside and sat up, wincing at the stomach muscles that screamed in agony with each motion.

She looked at Nero. "What have you done with Scarecrow and the Woodsman?"

"Oh how cute. You've given them names. The two automatons that accompanied you into my city have been entered into tonight's games. I must thank you. Attendance had started to wane. People were getting bored watching the same old bots beat each other up week after week. But with your two new contenders entering the mix…" He waggled a finger at her. "Tonight is going to be a packed house. I just know it."

"I didn't authorize you to enter my automatons into any games."

"I do not need authorization. If there is an automaton in my city, I take it. I only offer the reward so that people think they have a choice. They usually take the reward. Considering the alternative."

"What is the alternative?"

"Why bore you with local politics? You should get ready. Lunch is in half an hour."

"Return my automatons or…"

"Or you'll what?"

"I am the East Marshal…"

He cut her off with a raised voice. "And that means nothing here." He looked ready to continue his tirade, but then his demeanor shifted and his face softened. "One of the best ways to get people to do what you want, without question, is to give them a choice. You can either choose to be my guest or you can choose to be my prisoner. However, remember what I said, prisoners don't get the nice little chambermaid."

She stared at him silently, her fists clenched.

After allowing for a dramatic pause to let his point sink in, Nero smiled. "Excellent choice."

He headed out of the room. "Be sure our guest is dressed in something befitting someone of her station."

Alice spread her pale blue frilly skirt as she curtsied. "Yes, my lord."

The doors closed behind him and Dorothy was alone with Alice and, despite knowing otherwise, Dorothy still thought she looked completely human. Where did Nero get the technology to build an automaton that could pass for being human?

Alice smiled at her. "Your bath is ready, milady."

Dorothy grimaced from the pain in her side as she stood up. She walked slowly over to Alice. "May I touch your skin?"

Without any hint of concern, Alice lifted an arm up for her to touch. "If you wish."

Dorothy extended a finger and touched her arm. She jerked her hand back quickly in surprise at how soft and warm the skin felt.

Alice looked concerned. "Am I too hot? I can regulate my temperature to something cooler to make you more comfortable."

She shook her head. "No. I wasn't expecting you to feel so…"

"Human?"

She smiled at the little girl. "I don't mean to be rude. My father worked with lots of automatons when I was a little girl before they were outlawed. I don't remember ever seeing anything as advanced as you. Who built you?"

Alice turned away. "Your bath is getting cool and you are expected to be on time."

Nero strode into the large cavern carved out of the unforgiving earth beneath the coliseum. Repair bays lined both sides of the quarter mile long hallway. He surveyed the men in coveralls working on various gladiator automatons. He spotted the one he was looking for and walked over to stand next to him.

Nero regarded the latest two additions to his gladiator games. "Are the modifications complete?"

The elderly man, dressed in coveralls, wiped grease from his hands on a towel that looked dirtier than his hands. "The big one was no problem, but this new one," he motioned to Scarecrow with the dirty rag. "Never seen anything like it. It was hard to make heads or tails of the mechanics inside. And near as I can tell he was a clean slate upstairs."

Nero looked Scarecrow up and down. "Will he be ready to fight tonight?"

"Aye. I was able to make the modification, but I had to do a little tweaking with the design and gave him some rudimentary programming.

At this point, I can guarantee you, he will lose any fight you put him in."

Nero patted the elderly man on the shoulder, causing dust to lift from his coveralls. "Always open with a comedy act. It warms up the crowd."

Together, they regarded Scarecrow. His long overcoat and top hat were gone. Instead, he wore steel studded leather armor emblazoned with the Classical Greek letters "αγων".

The dark brown leather suit looked more impressive than it was. It provided no protection against the weapons used in the games. Its primary purpose was to provide a theatrical atmosphere for the games.

Scarecrow looked at Nero with a tilt of his head. "I take it by the word 'contest' spelled out in Greek on my outfit, I am to be entered in some form of competition?"

Nero laughed. "You are correct. Everyone who enters the games carries the Agon coliseum logo. You are the opening attraction tonight." He furrowed his brow. "I was informed that you haven't been programmed yet. How did you know the letters on your uniform were Greek and what they meant?"

"I contain a complete compendium of human history in my memory."

"Really? How strange, and somewhat useless. If you survive tonight, remind me to wipe all that nonsense from your brain to make room for some combat protocols."

"I do not belong to you."

"As far as you are concerned, I am your god and I will do with you as I please."

Nero picked up a tiny box with a single switch on it. He pressed the switch and Scarecrow immediately shut down. He moved in close and stared into the dark eyes of the disabled automaton.

He stepped back and smiled again at the silent Scarecrow. "Now that we've got that out of the way, I expect you to give my audience a show they will never forget."

While Dorothy had been bathing, her clothes were washed and laid out neatly on the bed. It had taken some convincing to get Alice to wash her Marshal uniform rather than make her put on the frilly dress she had originally laid out for her. In the end, Dorothy won her tiny victory and dressed quickly back into the leather corset and boots.

Dorothy followed Alice down the hallway. They passed ornately carved statues and oil paintings from the various art masters. She recognized some of the more famous paintings but could not remember the artists' names. She should have paid more attention during her school field trips to the museums. She wondered if any of these paintings hanging before her were originals and the fakes were in the museums outside of the Outcast Zone. This would be the last place anyone would look for stolen artwork.

Alice paused before a set of massive mahogany doors, inlaid with pearl, and looked at the man who stood guard. His face and arms were covered in a golden fur.

She remembered the young boy she had saved a couple years back and wondered if this was him. He refused to look at her and instead focused his attention on Alice.

Alice smiled at him. She still looked and behaved completely human. Dorothy shivered a little. This place was as far removed from reality as she had ever been. A young girl in a frilly dress named Alice was leading her through a veritable wonderland. The irony had not escaped her.

However, when the little girl spoke, she spoke with the wisdom of the ages. "Good day, Caleb. Mr. Nero has requested the Marshal join him for dinner."

I do have a name, thought Dorothy. She decided against saying what she thought aloud. Nobody she has met yet wanted to call her anything other than her new title.

Caleb smiled back at Alice; his sharp teeth glistened in the bright light of the hallway. "Good day to you, Miss Alice." He turned and opened the doors with a practiced grace. They swung open silently to reveal an equally massive banquet hall. The long table had at least a hundred chairs spaced evenly on each side. Only the head of the table and the chairs next to it on the far corner had been set with plates and flatware.

Caleb motioned toward the chair at the other end of the room.

"Mr. Nero will be in shortly. Please, have a seat." He bowed as he swung the large doors closed leaving Dorothy and Alice in the room alone.

Dorothy didn't move slowly, but it still took nearly a minute to walk the length of the table and reach the far end.

She turned back and noted that Alice stood off to the side of the large doors. Dorothy realized she would patiently wait as long as she had to before Dorothy was to be taken back to her room. It was unnerving that someone who looked so small and frail was her guard and who was more than capable of preventing her from escaping.

"Please have a seat, Dorothy."

She jumped and spun around to see who had snuck in behind her. Whoever this was not only knew her name but also actually used it.

She stammered as she spoke. "You... You know my name?"

Nero chuckled. "I know a lot of things about you Dorothy. But the only thing I'm interested in is your emerald necklace."

Dorothy instinctively reached for the necklace around her neck and found it still was not there. "I lost it in the crash."

He regarded her for a moment as he tapped a finger on his lips. "Most unfortunate. But I think you can still help me."

"Help you with what?"

He ignored her question and instead answered her with one of his own. "Do you know how I have managed to stay in power for as long as I have?"

She started to say something, but he held a finger up to silence her. "I know what you're going to say, and you're wrong. I'll let you in on a little trick of mine that I use to test those closest to me. Whenever I get that nagging feeling that someone is plotting against me, I pretend to be poisoned by my drink. I gasp and choke. Bulge my eyes out and clutch at my throat." He pantomimed his hands at his throat and bulged his eyes as he spoke. "Surprisingly, the more dramatic I am, the more convincing it is. As I lay dying, someone always takes that opportunity to gloat at my seemingly painful demise. It never fails."

"And what do you do with them once you've routed them out?"

He smiled, "They're never heard from again. And I am still top dog."

Dorothy looked at him. "I feel sorry for you."

He laughed. "Sorry for me? Why?"

"Because you do not have real power. Making people afraid of you is not power."

He grabbed her by the arm and herded her across the room.

His fingers dug deep into the muscles of her arm. "Ow! You're hurting me."

He shoved her toward the window and, for a moment, she thought he was going to push her out of it. He pointed down to a large fountain in the courtyard of the casino.

"The most precious thing in OZ is a clean glass of water to drink. I have an entire fountain of it, just for me to look at. That is true power."

She stared at him, her anger boiling just below the surface. "And you abuse this power to take whatever you want and hurt whoever you want."

He released her arm. "You misunderstand me, Dorothy. I use my powers for good. It is because of me that no one in Roma wants for food, clothing, or shelter. I give them the best life they can hope for in OZ."

"In exchange for what?"

"Loyalty, of course."

"I would think loyalty would be easy to buy in a place like this."

Nero frowned. "Easy to buy, not so easy to maintain."

"Maybe your heavy-handed techniques are not developing the proper kind of loyalty. As soon as I put on this Marshal star, Munch and his brothers gave me their undying loyalty."

"And for how long did they promise this devotion?"

"I'm sure it would endure."

Nero half smiled, a glimmer of surprise sparkled in his eyes. "They didn't tell you?"

"Tell me what?"

He pointed to the star on her chest. "The protection that star gives you has an expiration date."

"An expiration date?"

"The law states that when a Marshal gains their power by killing the previous Marshal, there is a seven-day cooling period during which the new Marshal cannot be killed. Otherwise, that entire region reverts to the control of the Wizard. Since nobody wants that, everyone abides by the law. By my calculations, you have about four days left before that shield becomes a huge target."

"What are you saying?"

"I'm saying that whoever has you at the end of four days, gets the star."

"Are they going to force me to give it to them?"

He smiled, but it was not a warm smile. "That's not how we do things here."

Chapter 6

Nero slid the chair out and helped Dorothy into her seat at the table.

"I do not mean to worry you dear. I just want you to be prepared for what's coming if the Wizard is unable to get you out."

She looked up at him quickly, obviously startled.

"You know I want to leave?"

"No one has ever attempted to break out of OZ without me finding out about it."

"Are you going to stop me?"

"I'm going to help you."

She stared up at him unsure of how to respond. Her eyes darted back and forth searching his eyes for the truth.

He smiled as warmly as he could.

"Because of my position, it cannot look like I am helping you. But you're going to have to trust me."

Before she could ask him the obvious questions that were most certainly burning in her head, Caleb opened the door and interrupted them. "I am sorry to disturb you, sir, but I have an urgent message for you."

Nero looked down at Dorothy. "I'm afraid I must a step away. Please enjoy your dinner and, when you're finished, Alice will take you back to your room."

He winked at her. "Remember what I said."

Caleb closed the door as soon as they were both in the hallway and looked at him with a concerned expression on his fuzzy face. "Do you think she understood?"

Nero stared at the closed door as if he could see right through it at the young girl who, literally, fell out of the sky and landed in the middle of the largest power struggle that would change the world forever.

He nodded to Caleb. "Make sure she understands."

Caleb bowed and walked swiftly down the hall and disappeared through another door.

Nero straightened his coat and strode into a small room off the main hallway. Inside waited a young man and an old man, both dark-skinned natives of this large continent.

As soon as the young man saw Nero he bowed respectfully.

"The Queen wishes to speak with you."

He laughed. "She's not the Queen yet. There is still much to do before that can happen."

The young man stayed bowed. "My father will be your conduit to the Queen."

Nero looked at the old man who was adorned with shells, bones, and feathers over his entire outfit.

"Why can't she just send me a handwritten letter like everyone else?"

The old man knelt down on the ground and untied a small leather pouch from around his waist. He poured a tiny pile of powder out onto the floor from the pouch. He clapped his hands together loudly once over the tiny pile and it erupted into purple smoke.

The smoke wafted up and encompassed the face of the old man who began to hum deep in the cavity of his chest.

"He is clearing his mind and getting ready to join telepathically with his brother who is in front of the Queen right now," said the younger man.

"I know what he's doing," replied Nero as he shook his head and reminded himself that he should have pushed harder to get the new electric telegraph system installed throughout OZ. It would be a lot more stable than the witchcraft the natives used.

The old man started to hum deeper and louder as he rocked from side to side. Nero remembered the first time he was told about the Australis natives' innate telepathic ability. He immediately discounted it as some form of belief system coupled with suggestive ideas that were so generic they could be construed to mean anything. He never really took much stock in signs of mysticism, or astrology, or seers.

Nevertheless, there was something different about these natives. They have proven repeatedly to be able to communicate specific details telepathically over large distances.

The old man suddenly went quiet, his eyes snapped open. The stark whiteness of his eyes glowed in direct contrast to his nearly charcoal black skin. "The Queen has canceled her trip. The girl does not matter. Only the star and what it represents. Give it to the princess when she boards the airship."

"What airship?"

"The Queen is sending her fastest airship. It will be here tomorrow morning."

Nero move closer to the old man.

"Tomorrow morning is too soon to guarantee getting the star."

The old man looked at him, but his gaze went straight through him as if he wasn't even there. "Do what I hired you to do Nero."

"West Marshal, you hired me to make you Queen of OZ. And that is what I plan to do."

"Very well then. I leave it up to you how to do it, but I want it done by tomorrow."

The old man dropped his head and it swayed from side to side. He let out a large sigh and then sat up. He looked around as if he was unaware of what had just taken place.

Nero smiled at the natives. "Thank you very much gentlemen, if you will make your way to the restaurant I will see to it you get a good meal before leaving."

They both smiled at the thought of eating the luxurious foods they had heard were served in the casino.

The two men left shaking his hand and thanking him gratefully for his offer. As soon as they left the room, he shut the door. He walked over to a marble bust of the original Nero of Rome and shoved it off its pedestal. It shattered into a several large pieces, a plume of dust emanating up from the chunks of marble.

Who did the West Marshal think she was?

Before he had arrived in OZ, the marshals had been unsuccessful in their attempt to overthrow the quasi-government of this prison-nation from the man everyone called the Wizard.

Not long after Nero's arrival, all of that started to change.

It had taken nearly seven years to break the Wizard's grip over OZ. Now, thanks to his tireless campaign, the Wizard had very little influence over anything outside the walls of Central City.

He stared at his reflection in the ornately carved mirror hanging on the wall.

Everything that happened up until now was because of him.

His work.

His plan.

The West Marshal was nearsighted. She could not see the bigger picture. Fortunately, for her, she hired Nero to handle the details, and he knew exactly what needed to happen next.

The first thing Dorothy thought of as she slowly emerged from a deep sleep was not remembering falling asleep. She remembered looking at the food spread out on the table before her and realized that, in a place like this, she wouldn't get another chance to eat this well. The last thing she remembered was feeling lightheaded and staring down at her plate wondering if eating too much could make you pass out.

The next thing she noticed was the dripping sound that echoed in the darkness.

The last thing she noticed was that it was dark because her eyes were still closed.

She fluttered them open and found herself staring at a simple stone ceiling rather than the ornately painted fresco in her room.

She rolled over to her side and saw thick steel bars made up the walls that contained her within a six-foot by six-foot area.

Someone spoke from only a few feet away. "Oh great. Looks like the princess finally decided to wake up."

She rolled over to her other side and saw Jasper staring at her from inside his own cage.

"Jasper? What are you doing here?"

"Probably the same thing you're doing here. Our automatons have been entered into the games and it's our job to fix them between battles."

She sat up quickly and suddenly wished she hadn't when the room spun. She winced and squinted at Jasper. "What do you mean our automatons?"

"Well, I couldn't collect the reward if I didn't say they were mine."

She shook her head and laughed sarcastically. "I can't believe I trusted you."

"I was going to share."

She looked passed Jasper at the massive underground cave. As far she could tell, they were the only two people inside cages. The rest of the people milling about seem to be repairing automatons or digging through piles of debris looking for parts.

None of this made any sense. The last thing Nero said to her was that he was going to help her. What he seemed to have actually done was lock her up in a cage under his coliseum.

Certainly not the kind of help she had expected. But then again, she reminded herself, she was still in the world's largest prison and truth was a commodity that was obviously scarce.

She stood up slowly allowing the room to stabilize before walking over and gripping the bars of her cage. Jasper watched her pull and push at the bars.

"Those are made from wootz steel. Ain't nothin' gonna bend those bars."

She ran a hand up and down one of the bars and inspected it closely. "It's not the bars that are the weak point. It's the man with the key."

She hollered out trying to get the attention of two men working on an automaton nearby. One of them started to glance in her direction but the older man immediately scolded him. When the older men returned to banging on the automaton with a crude hammer, the younger man quickly looked at her, smiled and shrugged his shoulders as if to say, I'd like to help but I can't.

Jasper watched her with interest and spoke up again. "I already tried that, but it looks like nobody's allowed to talk to us."

Suddenly, the constant droning sound that she had been unable to place increased in volume as massive doors on one side of the large underground cavern opened up. She quickly realized that the noise was the cheering crowds of the coliseum. There must be games going on right now.

The massive doors closed as soon as a man entered pushing a large cart filled with automaton parts. The cheering was muted again, but still audible as background noise.

The man noticed her watching him and called out. "Hey. You the one that brought the scarecrow?"

"Yeah."

The man pushed the cart over to her. "Do you think you can tell me if any of these might still be serviceable as spare parts?"

She looked into the cart and saw what remained of Scarecrow. He had been chopped apart at every joint and bend. Copper wires poked out the ends of every piece like bits of straw.

She looked up at the man. "What happened?"

"That had to have been one of the funniest show I've ever seen. The thing just stood there while the Woodsman hacked away at it. It almost looked like he fell to pieces at the Woodsman's feet."

She reached between the bars and started grabbing pieces of Scarecrow out of the cart and pulled them into her cage.

"You can't have any part of him."

The man watched as she removed every piece of Scarecrow out of the cart. Before she could grab the head, he snatched it out of the cart. "Don't hog all the good stuff."

She stared hard at the man. "Give me the head."

"No."

"Do you want to be the one to explain to Nero that I couldn't repair his newest automaton because you wouldn't give me every piece?"

The man nodded at all the parts piled around her feet. "Those things are destroyed. Look at them. There's no way you're getting that thing back together."

She held her hand out between the bars. "Not without the head I'm not."

Reluctantly, he slowly handed her Scarecrow's head.

She smiled. "Thank you."

The man grabbed the cart and waddled off, muttering to himself.

Jasper pressed himself against the bars of his own cage. "You really think you can fix that?"

She sat down on the hard dirt floor and started at all the parts. "No. But I couldn't see him being melted down for scrap."

Things were not going well for her. First her airship crashed, killing the only people who knew how to find her father. Then she lost the emerald that could help her find her father. Now she lost both automatons that were going to help her get to the Wizard, so she could get out of OZ and wait for her father to contact his group again.

She was locked in a steel cage in the middle of the world's largest prison and there was nothing she could do to change her fate.

She heard a faint raspy voice. She looked up at Jasper. "What?"

Jasper looked back at her. "I didn't say nothin'."

She heard the faint voice again and looked around her, but there was nobody else close by.

Oh great, she thought. Now I am going crazy. Maybe the stress of everything that had been happening over the past three days was finally catching up to her.

"Put... Together..."

Okay, she thought as she looked around. She definitely heard something that time. She looked back at Jasper. "Not funny Jasper."

"What's not funny?"

"Stop pretending to talk like a ghost."

"I'm not. What's your problem?"

She shot him a sharp look. "Just stop it, okay."

"Sheesh, you really are losing it."

She sat there staring at the parts and heard the raspy voice again. "Put... Together..."

She spun around and yelled at Jasper. "I said stop it!"

He held his hands up to show her they were empty. "I'm not doing anything!"

"Well then who's saying that?"

"Saying what?"

"Somebody's saying something. And you're the only one here."

"Maybe it's your stupid robot talking to you."

She looked down at the head in her hands and saw the eyes still had a faint glow to them. The lips moved slightly and said, "Put... Together..."

She screamed and dropped the head.

Jasper laughed. "I swear sometimes, you are such a girl."

She picked Scarecrow's head back up and look at it. "Are you still alive?"

The lips moved again and he said in a faint raspy voice, "Put... Together..."

Dorothy stood up and arranged all the parts to scarecrow on the floor in the proper order. Jasper strained against the bars of his cage. "What are you doing?"

She dismissively waved her hand in the air as she stared down at the broken parts. "Shh."

The copper wires sticking out of every part started to vibrate. They suddenly came alive and wrapped themselves like snakes around the copper wires sticking out of the other parts nearest to them.

They coiled tighter and all the different parts pulled together and reformed into the arms legs torso and head of Scarecrow. His eyes lit up brightly and he sat up suddenly. It was as if he had never even been torn apart in the first place.

He looked up at Dorothy and said, "That was most unpleasant."

Jasper pressed against the bars of his cage. "How did you do that?"

Dorothy gawked at the fully repaired scarecrow. "I don't know."

Scarecrow stood up and faced Dorothy. "It is part of my design function. To eliminate permanent injury, I can dismantle into component parts and reassemble myself."

Jasper started laughing. "He's our ticket out of here."

Dorothy looked at him unsure of what he was talking about.

He pointed to a set of keys hanging from a hook on the wall not too far away. "Tear

Scarecrow apart, toss him through the bars of the cage and let him reassemble himself out there. Then he can just get the keys and let us out."

She looked at Scarecrow. He looked back at her, no expression evident on his robotic face.

"I can't force you to go through that again. But it's an excellent idea."

"My purpose is to serve you. There is a lever in my lower back that will force my parts to disassemble quickly."

He turned around and pointed to his back. "Push right there."

She stepped up behind him, placed her fingers on his lower back where he had indicated and paused. "Does it hurt?"

"Just push it quickly."

She pushed on his back and heard a faint click as the lever depressed. Scarecrow instantly crumpled to the ground in several pieces, his head rolling toward the bars of her cage.

Jasper pointed as he cried out. "Dorothy! The head!"

She drove after the rolling head, smacking her own head against the bars just as it rolled between the bars, out of the cage, and out of reach.

She ignored the sudden flash of pain and pressed herself against the bars, reaching first with one arm, and then the next. The head wasn't just out of reach, it was several feet beyond her reach.

She sat back on her heels and rubbed at the forming bump on her head. "I can't believe it! I am such a dullard."

"Marshal," Jasper hissed just above a whisper.

She turned to face him. "Now what?"

He pointed furiously behind her. Her eyes followed where he pointed and saw a man in a hooded cloak approach Scarecrow's head. He was dressed entirely in black, from black leather boots to black leather gloves. In the semi-darkness of the underground cavern, the hood successfully hid the man's face.

He bent down and picked up Scarecrow's head. He spotted the keys hanging from the hook on the wall and walked over. He curled his fingers around the entire ring of keys with his gloved hand to muffle the noise as he lifted them from the hook and walked swiftly over to the door of her cage.

He pulled back his hood enough to show her the golden fur of his face. It had to be the same boy, otherwise he wouldn't be here now. She rushed to the bars with a smile. "Are you getting us out of here?

Caleb smiled, his sharp teeth still glistened, even in the dim light. "You saved my life once. I could never forgive myself if I didn't return the favor."

"Does Nero know you're doing this?"

He inserted keys one at a time into the lock and tried to turn them. Some refused to turn while others refused to fit in the lock it all.

"I can get you out of the casino," he said, as he looked her deeply in the eyes. "But promise to never tell anyone I was the one who helped you."

She looked just as deeply back into his eyes. "I will take the secret to my grave."

Jasper gripped the bars in his own cage. "Are you going to let us both out?"

Caleb glanced over at him and looked back at Dorothy. "Friend of yours?"

She grimaced. "Sort of."

Jasper's sweaty palms slipped on the bars of his cage. "I won't tell anyone you helped either."

Caleb struggled with the ring of keys, trying each one. He was running out of choices and not one key had unlocked the door yet.

There was a sudden loud clanking noise under her feet. She looked down and, for the first time, realized that the floor of her cage, including a walkway that bordered the entire circumference outside the bars, was made entirely of wood. Her stomach somersaulted as the whole cage lifted up quickly.

Caleb gripped the bars as he rode up with her through the ceiling and right into the center of the coliseum.

The cage jerked to a stop and she grabbed the bars to keep from falling over. Off to her left, a second cage rose up into view through the floor. Jasper's terrified eyes locked on to hers as his cage jerked to a stop.

The crowd went wild.

There was not a single empty seat in the entire coliseum.

It looked like the entire population of OZ was in attendance. It certainly sounded like it.

Several guards descended on Caleb and grabbed him as he tried to run.

They forced him to his knees as Nero walked up and regarded him with a disgusted look on his face.

Nero raised his arms and, in a matter of seconds, the entire crowd fell deathly silent. It was unnerving how 80,000 people could suddenly go quiet and collectively hold their breath.

Even though he addressed Caleb directly, he raised his voice loud enough for everyone in the coliseum to hear him. "When you were nothing but a helpless infant I took you in and raised you as my own son. You have disappointed me more than anyone else ever could."

Caleb struggled against the guards who held him down on his knees before Nero. "She saved my life. I owed her."

"And to repay this debt, you were willing to risk everything?"

"You taught me that honor and loyalty are commodities not easily ignored."

"Since you're so eager to share in the fate of your new friends, then I have no other choice but to let you."

Nero walked up to Dorothy's cage. She could sense the audience in the top rows leaning forward in their seats as they strained to hear what he would say to her.

She pressed herself to the bars of the cage and whispered, "You said you would help me."

He gave her a small wink and a sly smile before he turned around dramatically to address the audience. "I give you one chance to surrender the East Marshal star to me before I take it from your lifeless corpse."

What is he doing? It certainly didn't look like he was helping. Privately, he had promised to help. Publicly, he was demanding she relinquish the star to him or he would kill her.

Why would he do that?

Unless somebody was watching him.

That was it!

He had told her to trust him and that he couldn't make it look like he was helping her.

He was just making a good show of it.

Moreover, she had to help him make it a good show.

She lifted her chin defiantly and yelled, "I will never give you the East Marshal star."

He spun around and looked at her with a huge grin. "That's exactly what I wanted to hear."

The crowd went hysterical.

He held his hands up and quieted the crowd once again. "Ladies and gentlemen, for the first time ever we will have intelligent prey in the theater. For this special occasion, I have outfitted a Woodsman with a radio-controlled receiver. I will personally be operating the automaton and will thus be eligible to take credit for killing the East Marshal."

Dorothy's ears rang from the drone of the rabid spectators yelling and pounding their feet in anticipation of the spilling of her blood.

Nero held his arms high as he exited the coliseum floor to the adoration of his fans. As soon as he left, the soldiers shoved Caleb face down in the dirt and laughed as they departed and locked the exit to the coliseum battle arena behind them.

Dorothy and Jasper's cage doors unlatched and swung open on their own.

She ran out to Caleb and helped him back up to his feet.

He waved her off. "I'm okay."

Jasper ran up to them and pointed to the opposite end of the coliseum. "I don't think any of us are okay."

They watched as the Woodsman was raised up on a platform, much like they had been raised up from underneath in their cages. The platform jerked to a stop once it became level with the floor and the Woodsman shifted slightly from the change in momentum.

The speaker on the front of the Woodsman automaton crackled to life allowing Nero's modulated voice to be heard over the screaming crowds.

"Let the games begin!"

The roar of the crowd drowned out the whine of the chainsaws as they spun up to a blur.

The Woodsman proceeded forward. He was unsteady on his feet at first, but then he picked up a rhythm and headed straight for the small trio.

Jasper gripped Dorothy's arm. "What do we do?"

Dorothy stood frozen as she stared at the Woodsman bearing down on them. Her eyes were transfixed on the spinning chainsaw blades that got closer with each massive step the Woodsman took.

Jasper frantically shook her arm with both hands. "Marshal?!"

She snapped out of her frozen state and said the first word that came to mind.

"Run!"

They ran in different directions, which was exactly what she wanted them to do.

As she predicted, the Woodsman shifted direction to follow her and ignored both Jasper and Caleb. She ran as fast as she could and soon felt the ground tremble beneath her feet with each heavy footfall as the Woodsman gained on her.

She desperately wanted to twist her head to see what was going on behind her, but knew if she did, it would slow her down and throw her off balance.

The crowd's collective voice suddenly rose in excitement and she ducked just as a chainsaw cut through the air in the space where her head had been half a breath before.

She was beginning to doubt Nero ever planned to help her.

Jasper had only run a few dozen steps when he realized the Woodsman was going after the Marshal. He slowed to a stop and watched her run as fast as she could, but the Woodsman still got closer with each step.

When she ducked just before the Woodsman cut off her head, he knew he had to do something to help her.

There was no way a 12-year-old boy could stand up against a death machine more than twice his size. However, he couldn't sit idly by and watch it cut apart the new Marshal either. He had to figure out a way to even the odds somehow.

He looked around for any type of weapon he could use. Nero had not provided any weapons for them. It was obvious this was a one-way slaughter fest.

His eyes fell on the pile of scarecrow parts in the Marshal's cage. The Woodsman before had already torn Scarecrow apart easily, so there was no way he would be any good in a fair fight. However, Scarecrow was faster and more nimble than the Woodsman was. If he could convince it to pick up the Marshal and keep her away from the deadly spinning blades, they might last long enough to get a reprieve and have more time to devise an escape. He knew from attending past games that the spectators became restless when contestants stayed away from each other for more than ten minutes.

That was the problem with modern audiences, he thought. They always wanted to get right to the chase. If Jasper could bore the audience, Nero would have no other choice but to do something else. It was a long shot, but anything was better than what was happening now.

He ran back to the cage and began rearranging Scarecrow in a more recognizable form. He finished laying out the various parts when he realized he was missing the most important piece, the head.

He glanced around him and saw it lying several feet outside the cage. He leaped up and ran out to get it when the lion-man scooped it up and kept running.

Jasper called after him. "Hey! I need that."

The lion-man hollered over his shoulder. "Sorry kid, I need it more than you do."

Exhaustion was settling into every one of her muscles. She gulped for air and could feel her body winning out over her mind. I'm sorry father, she thought. I tried my best.

The crowd swelled with excitement and she ducked again, but this time no spinning chainsaw blade cut through the air above her head. She risked a peek over her shoulder and saw Caleb running straight for them. He gripped Scarecrow's head in his hands and quickly gained on the Woodsman.

He was shouting something to her but she could not make it out over the roar of the crowd.

It looked like he was yelling for her to stop.

He yelled again and this time she could make out that he was yelling the word stop.

She skidded to a halt and dove to one side as the Woodsman slid past her. It was bigger and heavier and couldn't stop or turn as quickly.

She rolled back onto her feet just as Caleb flew past her and leapt into the air straight at the Woodsman.

Being part lion, Caleb was able to fly through the air at over twice his own height. As he sailed in an arc straight for the Woodsman, he lifted Scarecrow's head above his own and brought it down hard onto a box mounted to the back of the Woodsman.

The box exploded in a shower of sparks and the Woodsman froze. Caleb landed hard on the ground and rolled back to his feet in a crouch, ready for anything.

The Woodsman turned and faced Caleb as the chainsaws ground to a halt. The crowd slowly grew as silent as the Woodsman.

The speaker on the Woodsman crackled to life as the Woodsman's modulated voice echoed throughout the coliseum. "You are accused of attempted destruction of government property. How do you plead?"

Dorothy called out. "I pardon his crime."

The Woodsman faced her. "Let me do my job."

"Your job is to do whatever I want."

The Woodsman stared at her with a single, unblinking eye. "What do you want?"

Jasper was at her side. "Tell him you want to get out of here."

Caleb was looking all around him at the coliseum. "The walls are made of stone and the floor is several feet thick before the cavern below."

Jasper pointed to the cages still raised up in the middle of the arena. "What about the cages?"

Caleb shook his head. "The controls are underground; we have no way of lowering them."

Dorothy studied the cages and then looked back to the Woodsman as an idea formed in her head. "We don't need to lower them. Everybody follow me."

As they ran back to the cage, she took Scarecrow's head from Caleb and handed it to Jasper. "As soon as were inside, rebuild Scarecrow."

The spectators became restless and people started booing and hissing because the entertainment had stopped entertaining them.

Nero's voice broke through the rumbling of the crowd over a loudspeaker. "And just where do you think you are going?"

As soon as they were all back inside the cage, Dorothy swung the door closed and looked up at Nero in his observation box. She yelled to be heard over the quieting crowd. "We are done playing your game. I suggest you lower us back down and let us go."

Behind Nero's easy smile, she could see the rage building up inside him. Nevertheless, he did not let that breakthrough to the surface as he spoke. "I'm afraid that wouldn't be fair to my customers. They paid to watch you die."

She smiled back and addressed the crowd as much as she addressed him. "Then I guess you owe them a refund." She pointed to the floor. "Cut right there Woodsman."

The Woodsman spun up his chainsaws and cut half of the floor away. The wood planks dropped 20 feet down to the cavern below.

Dorothy swung down through the hole and grabbed one of the chains that made up the pulley system that raised and lowered the cage.

She slid halfway down the chain when she looked back up at her ragtag group who all gawked at her through the hole. "Don't just stand there, let's go."

One by one everyone jumped down and grabbed the chain. Just as Dorothy hit the floor and moved away from the chain to let the rest slide down after her, the ground shook under her feet. She looked over as the Woodsman teetered a little to one side but then regained his footing. "You jumped?"

The Woodsman stared at her with that unblinking eye and raised his twin chainsaws. "I have no hands."

Scarecrow was the last to slide down. He was unsteady as he hit the ground and collapsed to all fours. She was instantly at his side and helped him back up. He was much heavier than she expected and Caleb rushed over to help.

As they steadied Scarecrow on his feet, Caleb pointed into the darkness off to one side. "I know a way out of here and into the city."

The Adventure Continues...

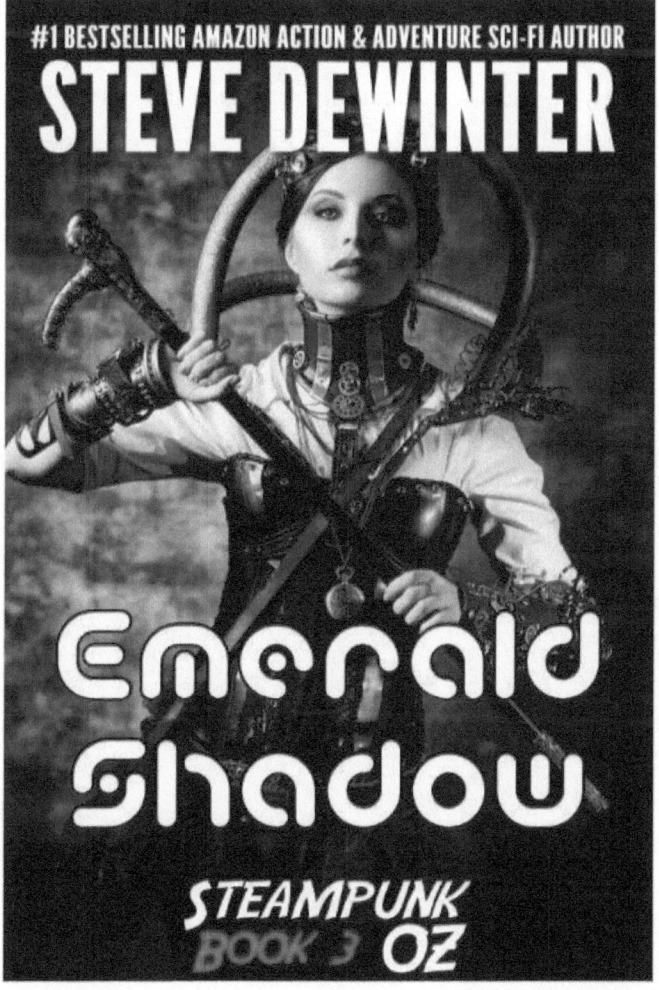

Sign up for Steve's Book Report (Mailing List) @ SteveDW.com
Know when his next book is released and other trouble he gets into ;-)

Other Books by the Author

A is for Apprentice (Fantasy)

Oliver Twist: Victorian Vampire (Fantasy)

A Tale of Two Cities with Dragons (Fantasy)

Shade Infinity (Science Fiction Thriller)

Peacekeepers X-Alpha Series (Thriller)
    Inherit the Throne
    The Warrior's Code

Steampunk OZ Series (Science Fiction Serial)
    Forgotten Girl
    The Legacy's World
    Emerald Shadow
    The Future's Destiny
    The Dangerous Captive
    Missing Legacy
    Shadow of History
    The Edge of the Hunter

Fugue: The Cure (Science Fiction Short Story)

Stay informed about all the trouble I keep getting into. Subscribe to Steve DeWinter's Book Report (i.e. the mailing list) @ SteveDW.com